The Many Shades of Light

The Many Shades of Light

First Edition

SHOSHANA AVNI

PARTRIDGE

A Penguin Random House Company

To order additional copies of this book, contact
Toll Free 800 101 2657 (Singapore)
Toll Free 1 800 81 7340 (Malaysia)
orders.singapore@partridgepublishing.com

www.partridgepublishing.com/singapore

Memories are more than recollected experiences. They're displacement of ourselves in time and space. They're events our younger self witnessed and participated in, recalled by older self who often wonders if he's truly the same person. They're visions of people we once knew.

—Robert Goddard

To my children Aya and Ur. May their lives be filled with many shades of light.

Acknowledgment

I would like to thank my very good friend **Rivka Eilon** for standing by me and encouraging me to write; My friends **Nisim & Sophie Ben Ari** for their lively impressions of South America; My good old friend **Regina Bruker in Rome** for her valuable comments; **Tali Inbar** and **Alina Ironi**, my young friends, for their enthusiasm and bright approach to life and last, but not least, to **Ms. Sydney Felicio, Publishing Consultant** in **Partridge**, for her hard work and dedication.

Chapter 1

Older Sarah

And now with all these new experiences of my older self, who is going to recollect them? Whose vision would I be?

I was way past my seventieth year when I first read Thomas Goddard's lines about memory. I realized at once that the images in those words had captured what I had once been, a young and vibrant woman who had loved and been loved. They did not apply to what I have been experiencing lately or to any recollected memories or experiences shared by people around me.

I drift between past and present, and I am not always sure whether I am fully awake or lingering in some ethereal limbo stage that has no boundaries of time, form, or place.

It first came to me early one morning when I could hear the whispering sound of dawn, though it was still dark outside. He was somewhere with me and around me in bed. I had a sense of something soft and very pliable surrounding me. I felt warm and relaxed and wondered whose short, sinuous fingers were caressing different parts of my body. At first it was only the tip of his long and strong fingers that touched my toes, and then each hand circled my ankles and pressed the flesh around them. Then he separated my toes and caressed the top cushions of each one as if they needed encouragement. Very lightly the fingers made their way up to my calves and thighs. They spread over the skin, felt the weight of the flesh, and moved on toward my groin.

It had been some time since I felt such an electrical jolt within my body. The sensation—and later the thoughts and memory of those long fingers that were close to what once used to be my core—were bewildering. My body stiffened, and I held my breath and wondered where it had come from and how I could still feel and anticipate any such sensations of pleasure.

The fingers stopped their explorations as if they were listening to me, and after a while they skipped to my navel and abdomen.

"Don't be startled, Sarah. I am here for you." It was a man's baritone whisper, a blend of voices I remembered from my past. I could almost tell who it belonged to—a round, warm, and loving voice I had heard so many times before. I craved it, but alas, it always eluded me. And I could never identify it properly anyway. The palms of the hands crawled to my breasts and lifted each one lightly and caressed each nipple in circular movements. Funny enough, there were no extra folded flesh or wrinkles around my abdomen. My skin was smooth, and my breasts were full and erect.

I could feel a slight weight of a light body along my back, but then it shifted itself on top of me and began its feral quest of my lips and face. My eyelids began to flutter before they opened; however, the fingers were sewing them with silky webs, and I returned to my ignorant bliss and sunk deeper into oblivion.

"It is nearly dawn. Can you hear the waves?" The airy weight slid down along my nipples and my abdomen and stopped there. Distant memories flooded my mind, and I held my breath and joined his rhythm in anticipation of what would come next. There was a light breeze and slight butterfly movements that slowly and delicately opened up the lips of my vagina and stopped there.

I was electrified, and the next moment I was filled with a mixture of sensations and thoughts. Shame came tangled with excitement. Fear was wrapped with mute giggles, and above all, there was amazement.

The memory of myself as young Sarah makes me smile. At this stage of my life it is easy and comforting to walk along memory lane, but I want to savor the new sensations my body is experiencing. It is common knowledge that most women my age have stopped experiencing them, or for that matter, they did not ever experience any kind of sexual arousal. Most of my friends would nod and smile when the subject came up. They would dismiss it with a wilted smile

I sit upright in my bed and wonder, *Am I mad? I'm in my midseventies and the last time I felt such thrill and excitement was ... some years ago.*

Now I remember the first time was when I was eighteen, just after my graduation from high school. Oh, it was a long time ago, and I have not thought about it for more than half a century.

Chapter 2
Young Sarah

It was late summer, and the air was sultry and damp. The sun had set an hour before, yet there was still light enough to see the beach and her house. She was dripping water from the swim in the stretch of sea near their house. It wasn't a private beach. It belonged to the whole community, but it wasn't officially guarded with a lifeguard, so it was fairly deserted.

She saw him standing there on the incline coming down from the house and just staring at her behind his dark Ray-Ban glasses. He was tall and slim. The very last rays of sun had lit his brown hair and tanned face. She knew at once he had been staring at her for a while, and something about his stance made her shiver.

She turned her naked back to him and looked at the sea and the horizon while something about the figure of the man kept niggling at her. She paused for a while and used the towel and T-shirt she had left on the beach to slowly dry herself.

She could feel his eyes boring into her bare back but preferred not to acknowledge his presence. He was just a casual passerby like many others each summer.

Now that she was nearly decently covered with her oversized T-shirt and towel, she turned around and walked the stretch of sand to the house. She had to pass by him, as the gate was her only point of entrance to the garden.

She had learned to ignore men's stares and the leers of strangers from an early age. Her friends at high school called her an "early bloomer," what with her firm boobs and towering figure, and the boys never let her forget that her presence bothered them without any provocation. She got the same reaction from strangers and family friends. So she simply ignored the stranger with a practiced aloof expression. She nearly made it, but suddenly his hand stretched out and caught her wrist. "Aren't you taking too far this skinny-dipping habit of yours?"

She could feel he was angry and excited at the same time, so she slowly gazed into his opaque lenses and calmly freed her wrist from his hold. "Did you enjoy it?" she asked.

There was a small smile of scorn on her face, and Sarah realized Ethan had picked on it at once. But it was too late as she heard her father, Joe Ketter, calling her from the porch.

"Oh, there you are, Sarah. I see you have met our guest. Come in, both of you, and have a cold drink."

"Don't you recognize this fine young man?" her father asked with a big smile. "Once when you were just in elementary school, you used to play together. Don't you remember? This is Ethan Saddot, the son of my friend from the air force." As she didn't respond in any way, he carried on. "You can't remember. You were too young, but you used to be on his back wherever he went. You wouldn't leave his sight, and when they left for the States, you cried for days."

Her father was beside himself with joy in the presence of this fine specimen of a man, but she was more reserved. Ethan had taken off his dark sunglasses, and she could openly look at his eyes. They were light topaz brown with green specks, and they were cold. He wasn't thrilled with her father's introduction, and she had little recollection of chasing him around the air base.

Her good manners and sense of humor came to her rescue as she approached him with a big smile and a stretched hand for a shake. He looked at her for a minute and realized he had to play along for at least as long as her father was present.

"Nice meeting you again, Sarah. I don't remember much about you chasing me around the base, but you have changed quite a bit."

"Thank you. Would you care for some cold drink? We always have a pitcher of fresh lemonade in the fridge."

He stood there deliberating her reply, but she could feel how his whole attitude had transformed once he had decided to play along.

At close proximity, he was quite tall. She was five feet nine, and Ethan was nearly six feet three with broad shoulders. He stood firmly on his feet, yet his movements were light and easy. *Maybe an athlete or a firefighter?* His hair was full and reached the collar of his pale blue shirt, and his jeans were well worn. He oozed testosterone, and on the whole he was quite a hunk, though easily irritated.

Her father monopolized the entire conversation. He asked about different members of his family, the electronic business his father had successfully developed, and his studies at Colombia University. Sarah felt good sitting and watching him squirm under her open gaze while her father grilled him about all and sundry, but after a short while she excused herself and went to take a shower and put on some decent clothes.

When she returned fully dressed with a sunny sleeveless dress, her long chestnut hair now dry, wearing pretty sandals, she found them still sitting there and earnestly discussing controversial football scores of their favorite international teams.

Her father gave her a quick look and said, "You look lovely, my dear. I'm happy you made it so quickly, Sarah. I have invited Ethan to join us on our weekly dinner. I hope you don't mind."

"Why should I mind? The more the merrier. Did you book a table?" Her reply was quick and followed with an impish smile.

He turned to Ethan and said, "I hope you like seafood, Ethan. We are going to a small trattoria along the beach. They have the best fresh seafood in the area."

Ethan replied quickly, "I love seafood. Is it considered an aphrodisiac here too, Sarah?"

"Do you need any inducement?"

Sarah could see at once that he was embarrassed by her flippant remark, and so was her father.

"Sarah, behave. You are not with your schoolmates now." He looked at her disapprovingly and then tried to excuse her behavior to their guest. "You see, since my wife, Mira, passed away three years ago, I am not at home much, and she is always in the company of her friends." Her father paused and then squeezed her shoulder with affection. "In fact, I am very proud of her. She never complains about me and David being away most of the week. She looks after the house and has graduated from high school with straight A's." He looked at her tenderly and kissed her on her head and patted her hair. "But sometimes she forgets her manners."

It wasn't a secret that since her mother had died from cancer when she was only fifteen, Sarah was left most of the time by herself. Her aunt, Rene, used to visit her quite a lot just after Sarah's mom's death, but she quickly realized that Sarah was an independent girl, and there wasn't much she couldn't do for herself. Her father was wise enough to hire the services of their regular maid, who had worked for them since before she was born, to come and cook and look after the house. Most of the time her brother was at university in the north, and her father was away on business.

However, they had this tradition of spending Friday evenings at home together, and any time her father went away, he would have dinner with her the night before. He was about to fly to South America the next day for two weeks, and her brother, David, was deeply involved with his semester exams. Joe Ketter was as tall as Ethan and quite lean. He was in his mid-forties and considered handsome by most women, but it seemed that though he accepted their interest in him, he was not prepared to open his heart to any other woman after the death of his beloved wife. Joe was athletic and loved to swim. Years before, he was a pilot, but since his service in the air force he had opened a small electronic company and traveled a lot. He had the same color of eyes as Sarah, deep gray, but they lacked the sparks that turned Sarah's eyes into the most prominent feature of her face. His light brown hair was turning into gray, which, in Sarah's opinion, made him look more distinguished.

Sarah was truly sorry for what she had said and so asked Ethan to forgive her. He looked at her with surprise, not sure whether she was pulling his leg again or not; however, her sheepish smile assured him she was earnest at least for the duration.

Chapter 3

The small restaurant was situated on a range of small limestone hills overlooking the quietly humming sea. The beach was partially lighted from above, and it was quite crowded at this time of the evening. Sarah had been to this trattoria many times with her family and friends and liked the simple decor. They were seated near the open windows and could hear the murmuring of the small waves kissing the golden sands. The square tables were covered with red-and-white-checkered tablecloths with colorful candles on each table, and the ambiance was intimate and friendly.

The meal and the wine were equally delicious and the fine breeze that came from the sea was welcomed instead of the heat and dampness of the day. The conversation went easily, and Ethan spoke about his parents, who had finally split up and had each gone with a new partner. He was quite a nice guy with a self-effacing humor, Sarah mused. She laughed from his vivid descriptions of his younger brothers' pranks and the awkward tackles with both his parents' new non-Jewish partners.

"Shirley, my father's better half now, is determined to learn all our Hanukah songs to please me, and Tom, my mum's current paramour, is keen to teach my mum the Yankees' colorful history in detail. He keeps asking her questions about them, but Mum is totally confused. It is very funny to see her want to please Frank."

Her father was happy with Ethan's company. Sarah knew he missed her mother dreadfully, and the fact that David was rarely at home didn't help the matter. She had realized quite early that as much as he loved her, she was no substitute for grown-up female company and conversations. She was still his adolescent daughter who needed tender care and love. It was difficult not to see how happy he was to discuss global and local business affairs or international sporting events with a grown-up.

Ethan, on his part, was quite knowledgeable yet patient enough to listen to her father's analyses of the world financial crisis. She sat there in a cool corner of the restaurant and listened to their voices. Her father's voice was clear and confident, and Ethan spoke quietly with a deep baritone that reminded her of a country singer.

Ethan's voice had a special timber. It was husky and measured, and she found it totally different from the voices of her male friends at school. He simply had a mature voice, and she was carried away listening to it and less to what he had been saying.

Suddenly Ethan stopped his conversation with her father and turned to look directly at Sarah. "What are you dreaming about, Sarah? Do we bore you?" He was looking at her in earnest as if he had been watching her for a while. He considered her embarrassment and continued, "Enough talk about money and football. I want to hear what you do with yourself all the time."

Both Ethan and her father were looking at her strangely, and she realized she must have missed some of their talk, which had been directed at her.

"What … what did I miss, Dad?" She was embarrassed and reluctant to be found out.

"I was telling you that since I am not going to be at home for two weeks and David won't be home much either, I suggested to Ethan he stay at our home instead of going to a hotel. What do you say?" Her Father was watching her closely while Ethan, his eyes half shut, had a little smile at the corner of his mouth.

Sarah knew she couldn't refuse her father's request and accepted it with grace and said, "You are most welcome to share our home, and I hope you won't be too bored here. However, you needn't worry about me because I am hardly at home, but of course it would be lovely to have you here."

"Oh, I am not going to babysit for you. I have a lot of work in the city and shall try to stay out of your way." It was clear that he sensed her reluctance that she didn't wish him to chaperon her at any time.

"I hope you will find time to go to dinner with Ethan once or twice, and what about that beach party you had planned for half the town?" Her father's message was loud and clear about her behaving cordially toward their guest. She smiled as warmly as she could and promised to go out with their houseguest on Friday evening.

As they got out of the restaurant, Ethan said, "Okay then, we have at least one date." He was all smiles, but she kept her council and returned to her reveries. He told her father he had rented a car, and so he left for his hotel in town while she and her father walked home along the beach.

"When are you going to find yourself a girlfriend, Dad?" The question popped out of her mouth, and she was as shocked by it as her father.

"Where has that come from, and why now?" Momentarily he couldn't hide his surprise, but soon after, he hugged her closer to himself and asked, "Do you miss Mum very much?" She felt like crying. It had been three years since her mother had passed, but she still missed her very much every day. However, there was nothing she could do about it, though she secretly felt her father was very lonely and needed female company.

"Yes, I miss Mother quite a lot, but I am busy most of the time with school and all my friends. What about you? Don't you want to meet any new women? You know you are very handsome and very popular with the ladies. They all inquire after you, and it is okay with us."

He was totally bewildered by her outburst. "Are you trying to get rid of me? What brought this on, and have you been discussing it with David?" He gave a long sigh and continued, "My god, my children are running my life." Then he burst out laughing.

"We talked about it only once when we saw you alone at Aunt Rene's party. There were so many women there who were interested in you. Even Aunt Rene said so."

He kissed her on her head. "Don't you both worry about your old Dad. I am fine. I will be all right, and I am not as lonely as I used to be. Now let's go home, and let me pack my suitcase."

Just before she kissed him good night, he looked at her and said, "Ethan is a good man, and I trust him to be a good friend." He looked at her closely and continued, "Now that you are no longer with Guy, why don't you go out with him? He is really good fun." He took a deep breath and went on, "I am not happy with this new situation with Guy. All this time he was with you, and now that you have split up, I worry you might be alone."

"It's okay, Dad. I am fine, and please don't worry about me." She gave him a big kiss and a hug and smiled happily. "We will be fine, Dad. Don't worry."

Chapter 4

The next day she met some of her friends from school, and it was funny to feel free to do or plan anything she wished. Finishing twelve years of school and passing all the final tests left a big hole in her life. She had no big plans for the summer because she was about to go to India with David and his girlfriend in the fall, so she just drifted from one beach party to another.

However, she did miss Guy. They had been friends for three years. He was a wonderful boy with golden hair and deep blue eyes. They did everything together and were the most popular couple in high school. The trouble was that Guy's parents had recently divorced and the father had left the house with two teenagers and a mother who had to juggle her time between a demanding job and the house chores.

The effect on Guy was hardly discernible at first. He accepted the change as a grown-up and helped his mother cope with his younger brother and the house chores; however, somewhere along the line something inside him had snapped, and he began to behave more recklessly, especially with his driving. And what was worse, he had started drinking alcohol with a group of new friends.

Sarah and Guy had planned to go on a trip to the south and drive along the new road that reached the big crater. They had been planning for months where to camp in the desert and the ride along some desert roads with some of their other friends.

However, the week before, she had told Guy she would not join him on the trip unless he promised her that he would not drink any alcohol before or during the drive and that he would keep within the speed limit. This was due to the fact that not long before, she had spent many months with her mother in hospitals and had seen many young *survivors* of road accidents. She knew she was not going to be part of this madness that had swept the country.

Every week there was news about more and more teenagers being injured or killed in accidents. Most parents had cars and let their teenage children drive without any adult supervision. Two of her schoolmates had gone on a joyride last winter and had skidded on the wet road. They were lucky to end up with just a wrecked car, neither fatally injured. When Sarah was in the hospital with her mother, they used to talk a lot about her friends, her studies, and life in general. She remembered once seeing a young female patient who was brought to her mother's ward and how it made her mother sad. "Please promise me you won't get involved in any silly and dangerous pranks. Life is precious. But it is also dangerous, and you should be careful," her mother had said.

Guy and Sarah had long arguments about driving fast, and eventually it reached a stage when Sarah stopped riding with him anymore. Finally they broke up. Sarah was sad about not being with Guy, but she was sure it was the right decision. Although she still loved him, it was not like it was before. She felt protective toward him but could not share his reckless behavior. He was looking for an outlet for his real feelings about his parents' breakup, and Sarah felt she could not help him by joining him in drinking alcohol and riding fast cars. She had spoken about it with her father and David, and they both agreed with her decision.

Sarah knew Guy was mad with her and tried to persuade her that his driving wasn't dangerous. Sarah was not surprised when Guy came to her house a few days before the trip to talk it over again.

"You know I'm a good driver, and I passed my first driving test before everybody else in class." He was really pissed off and angry because, like his parents, she didn't back him up on this issue.

"I know that basically you're a good driver, however—" and here Sarah paused for a minute and tried to soften what she wanted to say. "Lately you have started to drink in pubs and with new friends, so this makes you an unsafe driver in my opinion." She looked at his stormy face and tried to appease him. She put her hand on his arm and continued, "Look, the highway to the Big Crater is dangerous, and it has already been a scene of some fatal accidents. Why don't we drive, the two of us, to the north and go for hikes and swim in the lakes?" He pushed her hand away and stormed out of her house.

Sarah had not seen Guy for a few days and knew they were all going to leave the following morning. Sarah spent the day running some errands for her father and fixing details for the beach party.

It was early evening when Ethan returned home, and Sarah was already in the water. He gestured to her to continue swimming, and she was glad she had worn her full swimsuit, unlike the first time he saw her coming out of the water. He joined her on the rock and just seemed to unwind.

Sarah felt a bit uncomfortable near Ethan at first. She tried to fathom the reasons for her slight discomfort but could only come up with the sensation that he roused in her some strange and alien feelings that she was not familiar with. Sarah knew Ethan was attracted to her physically as a man, and his close proximity disturbed her.

Yet Ethan was a perfect gentleman, and their conversation was light and pleasant. He invited her to join him for a light supper in the nearby bar. It was easy to talk with Ethan, and he was earnestly interested in what she was involved in and her plans for the future.

"I understand from your father that your friends are leaving for a drive to the Big Crater in the south and you are not joining them. Why?"

He seemed to know about Guy, but she felt from the tone of his voice that he was sincerely interested to hear her side of the story, so she just told him they were all leaving on their trip the next morning and why she was not going to join them.

"You see, it was my idea to drive to the Big Crater once we both got our driving licenses, but that was before Guy began drinking alcohol excessively every day. And he does not want to promise me he won't drink before or during the drive." She did not look at him directly but could sense he was attentive to what she was saying.

"You know, I spent many hours and days with my mother in hospitals while she was sick, and I saw enough sick and injured people to last me a long time." There was sadness mingled with stubbornness in her voice. "I don't want to visit hospitals anytime soon, and I can't trust Guy to be reasonable."

Once again, although he seemed attentive and interested in whatever they talked about, she had a feeling he was preoccupied on a different level at the same time. Sarah was surprised that Ethan did not make any comments on what she had told him. He listened carefully to her reasoning, but she could not discern any reaction from his face or his eyes behind the dark glasses. Sarah sensed he was observing her from a different perspective, and she tried to shrug away the feeling. She said, "Well, I think we should head home. I am really tired." Sarah could see the first stars in the twilight sky and silently slid into the warm water. As they reached home, she went up to her room, and he stayed on the ground porch with his drink.

Chapter 5

From an early age Sarah could tell the time of day or the season of the year by listening to the waves. Living next to the sea, she had gotten used to hearing different noises than those she would hear in the city—the early gulls or the difference between the mall and big waves. There were other noises too, some seasonal and others attached to people who walked the stretch of beach below their house, and there were yet other noises. And though she was dreaming, Sarah identified those noises at once and with only one person—Guy.

It was nearly sunrise, and someone was throwing pebbles and sand at her half-open window. It could only be Guy. He had been doing it for years at odd hours of the day or night. Her family was aware of it, but all, apart from her, agreed to ignore him. She jumped from her bed to the window, and there he was, next to his parents' new white Volvo with tussled golden hair and sparkling blue eyes.

"Come down, sleepy head. Come down. I have already packed for both of us. Why aren't you ready? Did you think I would leave without you, golden girl?"

Sarah had not seen him for a few days, and her heart went out to him. She missed him so much. They had been mates for so long and knew so much about each other, yet she recognized the tone of his voice and the excitement in his eyes. Guy was not totally himself. She realized he was high and must have spent the night drinking with his buddies. She decided she had better go down and not let him wake up the whole neighborhood or Ethan for that matter.

She ran down with her flimsy T-shirt, and he caught her in midair and lifted her with his arms. He hid his face in her long, tussled hair and smeared her face with kisses.

"Come on. We are leaving. I missed you so much. I love you, and I want you to come with me." He mumbled and laughed, and there was an edge to his voice as if he would cry. His eyes were moist, and Sarah could discern a whiff of alcohol on his breath.

For a moment she thought of going with him after all, but first she had to talk to him. "Okay, calm down. I will come with you, but you must promise not to drive the car down the long, winding road to the crater and not drink." He looked at her with bewildered eyes and burst out laughing.

In an uncanny way Sarah realized it was a very important moment in their relationship. She did not enjoy their old pranks and mindless behavior anymore and wanted Guy to join her.

"Are you mad? Isn't that the whole idea of the trip? I want to drive myself and don't want you to tell me when I can drink." He was angry, and Sarah could see his feelings of frustration and dejection. "I am not promising you anything. If you don't want to come, then it's your decision. I'm going."

She stood there looking at him as he withdrew from her and walked to his car and kept looking in her direction.

"You know I love you." And as he got into his Volvo, he shouted, "Don't forget to wait for me. I am coming back for you."

Sarah stood there in the cool morning breeze and felt how her mind and body were kept on hold. Guy was gone, and she missed him already. Deep down, she knew it was the end of a wonderful friendship. She turned around and saw a shadow behind the blowing curtains in Ethan's room. He must have heard it all. In the kitchen he greeted her with a towel.

"Come, I'll race you to the rock. I think the cool water can be very comforting and pleasant at this hour of the morning." He didn't say anything else about the encounter with Guy, but she could tell he had heard it all.

Just once while they were lying on the rock, he lifted some hair from her face and smiled feebly. "You okay? Let's go back home, and I'll prepare a king's breakfast for both of us."

When he left for his businesses, he left behind him a detailed list of all the places he would be during the day with telephone numbers.

"I don't suppose you would call me, but anyway—" and he gave his self-effacing smile as he left the house.

It was a humid and sultry day, and Sarah was listless and in a funny mood. She didn't feel like doing anything, and yet she kept her mind and body occupied and busy the whole time. She met with some friends and organized a small local band to attend their beach party and mostly stayed indoors, but from time to time she thought about Guy and what he was doing. She was anxious but not sorry she did not go with her friends. The long drive and the winding road to the Big Crater did not appeal to her as much as before.

Her thoughts also wondered to Ethan, and she thought of how in a short time he had inserted himself into her life. He was quite attractive with his broad shoulders and the pensive look in the eyes, and though he did not talk about himself much, she felt he could be a good friend. Her father liked and trusted him implicitly. She felt she could talk to him about stuff she did not discuss with her brother or her father—stuff about her decision not to go on the trip, about what to do in life and how it feels to immigrate to another country and begin your life again with new friends and studies and divorced parents. She soon lost her initial reluctance toward him and was rather curious to know more about his life.

As she was pottering around the house, she turned on the radio for some music and then she caught the tail end of the news. The broadcaster finished his item with "a tragic accident" and "what a waste."

The broadcaster continued with some other matters of the day, and she frantically searched the other stations for more details. On the next station she heard some more. "The accident had occurred in the late morning around the Big Crater, and there were serious casualties." Sarah froze on the spot, and her mind went to Guy and her friends.

She immediately called David, who used to volunteer in the police, but he was not available, so she left him an urgent message to call her. Ethan's list was in front of her, and it was the most natural thing she could do. *I need Ethan. He can help me.* He answered her on the third ring.

"Ethan, there was an accident in the south with some casualties. Can you find some more details for me?"

"Why? Do you think it is Guy?"

"I don't know, but I have this horrible feeling that it is his car. You see, they said on the radio that they were driving a white Volvo, and Guy took his parents' white Volvo."

His voice was calm and embracing, and she didn't need to tell him anything else. He had witnessed the whole encounter with Guy in the early morning.

"Sit tight. I'll be home soon. I am not very far."

Sarah went out and waited for him until she heard his car in the driveway. He got out of the car, and from his stance and posture she could tell he was tense. She stood still and waited for him, and once he embraced her in his arms, she let her tears flow and gasped for air.

He held her close to him and spoke to her quietly. "I called one of my father's friends who is an executive manager of one of the radio stations, and you are right. It could be Guy's car. There were three passengers in the car—the driver, one passenger next to him, and someone at the back who was asleep."

Ethan put his arm on her shoulder and led her into the house. He looked into her bewildered eyes for a moment and then pulled her closer to him.

"I was told it was very quick and inevitable." He paused for a minute and then continued, "Do you know the registration number of his car by any chance?"

She lifted her head and nodded yes. He took out of his pocket a piece of paper and handed it to her.

Sarah felt her heart break, and she just let his shirt get wet with her pouring tears. She couldn't imagine Guy in any other form or shape but standing there in the morning light and promising to come back. Ethan said nothing. He just passed his hand on her hair and let her body sag into his embrace.

A car stopped outside the house, and Ethan told her it would probably be her brother, David. Ethan had known David from the time before Ethan's family had left for New York, and later whenever David went to New York, he visited Ethan too. He asked him to find more details from his friends in the police force. David was with his girlfriend, Mira, and once they caught sight of Sarah, they both just held her close and let her cry her heart out. When she eventually calmed down a little, David caught her face in his hands and gave her some more facts.

"I spoke with my friends in the police and verified the news you heard on the radio. Ethan tells me that you also verified Guy's car number." He paused for a long time and just caressed her hair.

"I don't know who the driver and the female passenger next to him are, but it was guy who was asleep at the back. He wasn't driving at all, and he didn't feel the crash with the oncoming tanker on the other lane. The winding road was slippery and sharp, and the crash was just inevitable."

She lifted her imploring eyes to her brother, and in a chocked voice, she asked, "You mean to say that Guy was not driving his own car that he was sleeping the whole time the car crashed into the tanker?" She sounded so incredulous and shocked. She went on to look into space and murmur to herself. "So Guy did listen to me. He did not drive." The news seemed to make her very sad, and she once again burst out crying while the news kept churning in her mind.

The news was bewildering. Guy wasn't driving; he was sleeping, doing exactly what she had asked him to do. Why didn't he tell her so in the morning? It didn't matter anymore. Guy was dead.

Chapter 6

The rest of the day was a blur. They tried to catch her father, but he wasn't available on the phone, so she couldn't talk to him. And her mother wasn't there anymore. However, she wasn't left alone for a minute. She didn't want to go out onto the beach because she did not want to meet people. She sat between David and Ethan on the couch and listened to them reminiscing about their childhood pranks and adventures on the air force base. Mira was in the kitchen, and with David's help she did the shopping and put some late lunch on the table. Sarah could see how tense they were not only because of her grief but also because they both faced final exams and had to study. However, it was Ethan she talked to most because she did not have to tell him about the last scene with Guy in the morning. He had been there and could see her anguish as the early morning scene flooded her mind every time. Ethan also told her a little about his intention to live in the Far East and his attraction to Eastern cultures. He told her he had studied engineering but wanted to take a break and maybe go climbing in Nepal.

Sarah noticed he did not share with her any personal information, but his deep, warm voice lulled her into some level of calm. He kept her company till she went to bed, and when she woke up weeping in the middle of the night, it was Ethan who had been sitting next to her on the bed and holding her. He told her not to hold back anything, to cry as much as she needed and talk about Guy. He told her to take comfort in the fact that Guy hadn't woken up before the crash and had not been responsible for the accident after all. She had nearly used a whole box of tissues, and after a while his soothing voice put her back to sleep.

When she woke up again, there was light outside and a soft breeze from the sea. Her brother had brought her a strong cup of coffee. He told her he had spoken to their father, and as they had agreed upon before, he had asked him not to break his trip because the funeral was on the same day and she wouldn't be left alone.

The cemetery was full with the school student body, the school management, parents, and many townspeople. Her friends, who surrounded her since the morning, seemed to need her more for solace and comfort than she needed them. The ceremony was deeply moving, and as all three victims were local students, there were many eulogies and poems read in their honor. The school choir sang some hymns, and many of the students openly wailed the tragic passing of their friends. For most of them it was their first and only encounter with death, and they found it hard to absorb a triple death. Sarah stood still and tried not to choke on the grief and agony that engulfed her. She looked at the grief-stricken faces of her schoolmates, their parents, and their teachers and realized this day would be different from the rest of her life. She would never be the same again. It cut her from her carefree youth and hurled her into the reality of real life. Among the whole congregation, she was closely surrounded by her brother, Ethan, and Mira and was thankful for that. She spoke a few words to David, and it was the most difficult thing she did when they all approached both Guy's parents. She embraced all of them and was engulfed by their love and deep grief.

She refused to join the many other mourners after the service and went directly to her home in the embrace of her family. She needed distance from exuberant displays of pain and grief of others. Sarah had David, Mira, and Ethan give her comfort in their silence.

The days passed by without any special events. After talking it over with her father on the phone and with Ethan in person, David and Mira left for their studies and final tests but kept calling her several times a day. Sarah refrained from going outside her home, and during the days her friends came to the house and filled it with their talks about the accident and reminisced about school trips and parties from the past when they had fun and were happy. Most of the time Ethan was not at home when her friends were there; however, each morning he would go to the nearest grocery and buy enough fresh rolls, eggs, dairy products, and soft drinks for her visitors. He would call her from wherever he was and ask her if she needed anything.

"Did you sleep well, and do you need anything?"

It was always the same, and she would normally put on a brave face and answer cordially, "I am fine, and don't worry so much." She paused for a minute and then continued, "Thank you for all the food and goodies you left in the refrigerator. My friends want to know where you sprang from and whether they can borrow your services."

He could feel she was smiling and answered her in jest too, "Tell them I provide my priceless special services only to very special people." At first Sarah felt a little odd to talk to Ethan and tell him about her everyday activities, but after a few days she felt comforted by their talks and could confide in him more.

Standing on the porch and looking at the sun sinking into the shimmering expanse of water had a numbing effect. Sarah knew it would take her time to absorb the full impact of Guy's loss, but at the moment she needed to blunt the deep gnawing pain in her heart. She turned round to get her swimsuit, and there was Ethan waiting with a towel. Sarah gave him half a smile and went into the house to change clothes. When she came out to the waterfront, Ethan stretched his arm to her, and she silently joined him in the water. It was good to swim in the fresh water and clear her head from everything. She had spoken to her father, and although it would have been much easier with him around, she assured him that David, Mira, and Ethan were doing their best to help her and there was no need to return home at the start of his trip.

Ethan was stretched alongside her on the warm stone, and she felt grateful for all he had done for her, especially his calming presence, but she left it unsaid. She just smiled at him shyly. He smiled back and squeezed her hand.

"I have decided to take some days off and travel to the north." He didn't look at her or raise his voice. He just casually suggested she come with him. "I have a friend who is digging some ancient fort up in the mountains, and I promised to visit him and his site." He paused for a moment and then continued, "He is a great guy and very interesting. You two would like each other." He said it with half a smile, and she didn't ask him why but just smiled back.

"Robin is a big baby with a brilliant mind. He could be a rocket scientist or a gifted musician, but he decided he wanted to dig up the past. And he has been excavating in different continents." He continued, "His university lectures are packed with students and groupies, and now he is digging here. He has a great sense of humor and loves young beautiful women."

Sarah looked at him inquiringly, and he continued, "In fact, I have a packet for him from his department, and he has asked me to look at some engineering problem he has come across.

I understand he needs to build a kind of support for an ancient cave, and he wants my opinion." He searched her face and asked, "Would you mind very much? We can stop anywhere you wish and just take it easy."

"What a good idea. I would love a change of scenery for few days. Just let me tell David about it."

It seemed to Sarah that Ethan had to impart all this information to her so that she would be ready, but nothing prepared her for Professor Robin Ford from Colombia University.

Chapter 7

They had traveled for two days in the mountains and followed some wooded trails. Ethan was a competent driver, and he seemed to know all the right roads up north. At first they drove along the coastal road and found small bays where they could swim and snorkel safely. Sarah wanted to visit the new alligator farm everybody was talking about and swim in the thermic pools. They slept in the open and took their meals at small motels.

Every evening Ethan built a bonfire, and they boiled water for coffee and rested from the day. Sarah told him about her school excursions and trips while Ethan listened to her silently, which she didn't mind. In fact, she liked his calm presence next to her and fell into a deep sleep the moment she put her head down on the sleeping bag.

When she arose with the first rays of the sun on her face and the sound of the crickets, she saw Ethan preparing coffee on the bonfire. Sarah noticed he was very handy and liked it.

On the third day they approached the dig along the coastline where Robin's camp was situated. From afar Robin looked like one of Sarah's mates from school. He was fairer and shorter than Ethan and very thin. He wore khaki shorts and a nondescript black T-shirt with a logo that said, "You are lucky to know me." His freckled face and shock of red hair were very distinct, but his small piercing black eyes with deep wrinkles around them were what captured her attention most. As they approached the dig, he took off his red bandana and wiped his face.

Ethan and Robin embraced each other like old friends, and then Ethan introduced Sarah to Robin. "I would like to introduce to you my friend Sarah Ketter." It was difficult to discern Ethan's exact mood from behind his dark lenses, but Sarah had a sneaking feeling that he was laughing in his mind.

"I heard you were beautiful, but this is unfair," was the first thing that Robin said.

Robin caught both Sarah's hands, and after a slow, intense examination of her long, tanned legs, her firm breasts, and then her hair and eyes, he held her face with his dusty hands, squeezed her to his body, and kissed her soundly on her lips. Sarah stood frozen, as she didn't know what to do. She could hear Ethan growling something, and then Robin released her abruptly.

"Don't let her be alone with me. She is too dangerous for my blood pressure." He burst out laughing and then introduced himself and his crew to them. Sarah became aware of how momentarily Ethan had tensed, but she could not read his eyes behind those opaque lenses. She just touched his shoulder slightly, and he seemed to get her signal. She was not offended, and she was okay. The crew seemed happy to have a short respite from their work and took Robin's outburst casually.

Once Sarah had overcome her initial shock, she found Professor Robin Ford fascinating and endearing at once. They were digging around an ancient Crusader's fort, and Robin's theory was that the area was a major compound where the Crusaders had their food depots and training base. He was full of enthusiasm about finding some significant artifacts and tools to confirm his theory and asked them to join him under the shade where most of the findings and restorations were being held.

Sarah could see that Robin and Ethan liked each other and were happy to meet again. She wandered around the excavations with one of the assistants and was fascinated with his explanations and theories; however, at one point when there was less light and the sun was disappearing behind the mountain range, she let Ethan know she was tired and wanted to leave. There was a small lake an hour's drive from the dig, and they intended to spend the night there.

The parting from Robin and his crew was friendly, and Ethan kept her next to himself for safety sake. Sarah could see Robin measuring them with a sly smile, but he just shook her hand and wished them a good trip. Both Sarah and Ethan were pensive. Sarah wondered whether Ethan had said anything to Robin, and Ethan was wondering whether he was getting too close to Sarah.

Chapter 8

It was already dusk when they reached the lake and booked themselves in a guesthouse. Their rooms were clean and simply furnished, and Sarah could take a long shower to wash off the long day's dust and heat. It was wonderful not to sleep in the open and to feel clean and fresh after the long drive and grueling heat. She wore a light summer dress, and Ethan was in some faded jeans and T-shirt. She felt relaxed and happy to see Ethan smiling at her.

It slowly dawned on her that in the last few days he had gradually become an important figure in her life, and it felt good. Sarah knew that although she had known Ethan for only few days, he had been next to her when Guy last visited her and the whole time since then. She shared very critical moments with Ethan and didn't have to talk to him about what was on her mind. He simply knew, and his calm presence added to her feeling of being safe. He put his arm around her shoulder, and they both walked bare feet out into the warm evening. The small pebbles on the bank felt warm under their feet.

They had been circling the lake when he suddenly asked her, "Did it upset you when Robin kissed you on your mouth?" Ethan looked at her for a moment with a blank expression and continued walking and talking. "I am sorry I did not prevent it, but it took me by surprise too. You must have impressed him greatly, more than the usual." He stopped walking and smiled wryly.

"Anyway, he did apologize to me and asked me to convey his regret if he offended you."

Sarah contemplated the incident for a while and realized she wasn't offended as much as bewildered from its suddenness.

"He simply surprised me. If he had asked for a kiss, I might have kissed him myself, for he is quite attractive in a funny way, but I don't like any kind of forced intimate acts." She paused and considered it further.

"He invaded my privacy, and I don't approve of it. But it is okay. I think he is harmless."

"And do you like to be kissed?" Ethan kept his arm on her shoulder, but she could feel his body tense up. This was a whole new territory for both of them, and she wanted some time to think it over. Sarah was quite honest with herself and knew there was strong attraction between them. She got excited by his proximity, his touch, and his smell and found him appealing in a grown-up way, but she didn't want to toy with him. He wasn't a boy, although she loved teasing him a little.

She paused and smiled at him. "Are you proposing to kiss me?"

"And what if I do?" He was so serious and tense that she burst out laughing. His expression changed instantly. He looked offended, and she immediately felt contrite.

"I am sorry. I didn't mean to offend you. This is all new for me, what with everything else. I am a little confused at the moment, but as to your question—" She had that certain glimpse in her eyes, and she said, "Well, I would love to kiss you though." And there and then she planted a swift kiss on his lips. But as she was trying to withdraw from him, he caught her face in both his hands and planted his lips on hers. At first it was a little demanding, but then it turned into a flow of soft and caressing acts that took her breath away. He gently parted her lips with his tongue and sucked her breath into his mouth.

She instantly knew that they had crossed a certain threshold and were heading somewhere new and different. Her arms went around him, and his whole body sagged into her stretched, supple body with relief.

"I have wanted to do this from the first moment I laid my eyes on you down on the beach, but it seemed so improbable." He pulled her with him to one of the trees along the bank and leaned against her while he stroked her hair with his fingers.

He anxiously looked into her eyes and seemed to be wary of her reaction. "Are you okay with this?"

She knew what he meant—the proximity of Guy's death, her being younger than him, and the fact that he was supposed to be her guardian. But she didn't want to think about any of it.

It was so good to feel his long, strong fingers going through her hair, the length of his body on her breasts, and his immediate arousal. She leaned on the trunk of the tree and just smiled at him.

Sarah savored this whole new world of sensations she had not experienced before. She had engaged in sexual play with Guy many times. They had both swam naked in the sea and felt free to touch and caress each other, and although they had gone the whole way, this was nothing like what she had experienced before. There was a tacit agreement between her and Guy that one day soon they would go the whole way properly.

Ethan's kisses seemed to have removed some unknown dam and opened the gate for a flood of new feelings and sensations Sarah had never experienced before. She could see the change in Ethan. He looked at her as if she were some unexpected and fragile phenomenon. Sarah surmised Ethan must have had experience with women and must have left quite a lot of broken hearts behind him in his life because of his good looks, but it seemed to her that she was something he had not bargained for and was shocked to discover that in just few days she had completely shattered all his reserves and rules of engagement with women.

From the first moment he saw her naked Amazonian body emerging from the sea, he was captivated. She had captured his mind and thoughts and rendered him helpless and confused. Holding her long and lean body close to his and feeling her full breasts pressing into his chest and bulging groin was much more than he expected when he asked her about kissing.

It was only after Robin had shamelessly kissed her did Ethan realize how possessive he had become of her in such a short time. Her big lustrous gray eyes were pinned on his face, and she seemed to be at ease with all the turmoil and excitement she had aroused in him. From her thudding heart and the tense hold she had on his shoulders, he could see she was aroused and excited too, but what amazed him most was her inner serenity and quiet.

He wasn't sure whether she had had any prior sexual experience, and with the way he felt around her, he was rightly worried; however, she seemed to be taking the whole switch in their relationship very naturally and almost casually. She seemed to be fascinated with her role in this new development between them.

Ethan reflected on the possibility that Sarah might not have been aware of her impact on men, but it was fine with her, as she equally seemed to enjoy her interest in him.

For a moment Ethan reflected that he had to draw back and be the responsible adult between them. Looking into her big trusting eyes, he surmised she couldn't have been aware of the kind of dilemma she had posed for him. On the one hand he wanted her desperately—to bury his face in her hair, to touch every inch of her skin and body, and to kiss her so thoroughly it would blunt the ache he felt in his whole body—but alas, she was still only a teenager and had just gone through a serious trauma. What compounded the issue was the fact that her father had entrusted her to him.

"You are quite a good kisser," she said and smiled. "I would like to practice some more." Her smile turned challenging, and he felt he had to stop it at once or else.

Reason prevailed, and Ethan said, "Aren't you hungry? I am famished. Let's go back to the guesthouse and eat. You must be tired." She let him pull her from the tree and wrap his arm around her waist.

There was a small restaurant attached to their guesthouse, and most of the visitors to the lake were already dining. Ethan noticed how all heads had turned to look at them and how attractive and young Sarah looked. He felt both joy and pride mingled with despair crawl into his heart. He turned his head and smiled at her because there was something beguiling and innocent about her despite her impish facetiousness.

The meal was simple and delicious, and they both enjoyed it with bottles of cold beer. There was a call waiting for her in her room from her brother, and she got the latest news from her father, who was having a wonderful time in the area of the majestic Iguassu Falls between Argentine and Brazil. He had sent her his warmest regards and love. David was happy to hear she was feeling good and enjoying the trip. There was a short talk between Ethan and David, and they decided to go to their rooms. Just before they parted, Ethan gave her a light kiss on her hair, and she smiled at him her enigmatic smile and thanked him for a lovely evening. He wasn't sure whether she was being facetious or simply didn't want to talk and just wished him good night.

Chapter 9

Ethan woke up at once, and though he knew it wasn't morning yet, he rose and went to the window overlooking the lake. If he hadn't known the lake was in front of him, he wouldn't have been sure about it because it was covered with thick fog that lifted from time to time to give short glimpses of dark stretches of water. He reflected on the varying events of the last day and wondered how Sarah saw it all. She was an incredible young woman who had gotten under his skin in just a few days and left his body and mind tense and occupied with her the whole time. He felt wide awake and decided to go for a swim despite the fog.

It was cool outside, and as he walked along the bank, he came across a fresh bath towel that looked familiar. *It couldn't be. Sarah could not be in the water. It was too early, and yet she could do it with her deeply ingrained love for swimming.* He swam quietly and looked for her among the dispersing moths of fog. After he spotted her, he swam quietly underwater and decided to surprise her. Sarah was floating on her back and seemed to be asleep. He didn't want to frighten her, so he just lifted her gently out of the water and turned her around to embrace her. Her reaction was extreme and unexpected.

Sarah was startled and dazed. She gasped for air and began struggling with him. Ethan realized it was wrong to have come upon her so suddenly and tried to calm her down. "Sarah, it's me, Ethan. Don't worry. I'm sorry to have startled you. Calm down, sweetheart."

He kissed her on her brows and held her tightly to himself. Once she realized who he was, she started crying soundlessly. She clung to him like a desperate child.

"Why? What happened? Have I frightened you so much? Why are you in the water so early and with so much fog?" He kept talking to her until her sobs subsided.

Sarah lifted her head from his shoulders, and her eyes were filled with deep sadness and anguish. "I couldn't sleep, and then I dreamt about Guy and how I would never be able to tell him I am proud of his decision not to drive and how much I miss him." She half-murmured the words into his neck and half-spoke to herself. "He is dead, you know. He is dead—"

"Yes, sweetheart, I know he is dead, and you should cry for him as much as you want. Come, let's get out of this fog and get dried. You need something hot to drink and some warm clothes." She let him pull her out of the water and wrap her up with her towel.

Ethan was greatly disturbed by her state of mind. Gone was the poised, young coltish woman who attracted him so entirely lately and bewitched his soul. Instead he held this fragile young girl who had lost her mate and had no parent nearby to comfort her and offer solace. For a moment he felt lost and looked at her in bewilderment, but though she looked so forlorn, she still looked beautiful and desirable. He wanted to keep her in his arms and cover her with kisses and wipe the anguish out of her eyes.

After she drank a cup of coffee and put on some light clothes, Sarah felt warmer and more comforted. The day before was quite eventful, but her night was really rough. She kept falling in and out of snatches of nightmarish dreams that featured only Guy. He was swimming with her, playing ball, studying with her for tests, kissing her, and then there was his lonely, crushed body lying at the bottom of the ravine. And only his lovely face and golden hair were intact. She couldn't bear to rerun those scenes in her mind anymore and decided to put an end to the dreams and find some rest in the lake water.

When Ethan lifted her so abruptly out of the water, she was half asleep and trying to shut out all those painful scenes from her mind. Ethan's hold took her back to the monster of Loch Ness and how scared she had been when her family visited Loach Ness in Scotland. She remembered her father holding her the whole time they walked around the lake and looked for the monster.

Ethan's sudden, strong hold on her waist made Sarah feel immediate danger, and she wanted to scream; however, Ethan's soothing voice, compassionate face, and strong arms penetrated her befuddled mind, and she sagged into his strong embrace and just let go. She began to cry and release the pent-up tension from her body.

Good old Ethan—he was so dependable and good for her. It was wonderful to cuddle up to him and feel his warmth next to her on the bed. Yes, she needed some sleep, and Ethan would be there when she woke up. As Ethan was stretched on the bed next to her, she buried her face in his arm and went to sleep.

Sarah woke up after a couple of hours of deep sleep and felt refreshed. The room was still dark, but she could see the light of dawn behind the heavy curtains. She felt Ethan's arm stretched over her warm body and smiled. Her own body was rested, and her mind silently recalled her night dreams and early morning swim in the foggy lake. It was Ethan who had taken her out of the water and put her to bed. It was his strong body that kept her warm, and now he gently turned around and looked into her eyes.

"Good morning, beautiful, did you sleep well?" He pulled her soft body to him, and long strands of her chestnut hair spilled over his face. He smiled at her. He searched her face for any telltale signs of the night before, but her big, lustrously beautiful, gray eyes were bright and pinned on his eyes with wonder. Her full, generous lips were parted and he couldn't resist her anymore. He held her head with both his hands and put gentle kisses on each lip and then kissed her full mouth and inhaled her body scent. She hesitated for just an instant but then put her fingers into his unkempt hair and returned his kisses. She could feel the whole length of his body tense up along hers, and it enthralled her. He made her feel alive and every muscle in her body craved his touch. Suddenly she became aware of his arousal, and it excited her.

Ethan was lost. He wanted her more than anything and found her fresh and guileless enthusiasm irresistible. He kissed her eyes, her brows, her lips and sucked in her breath. His hands left her face and traveled to her body. Her firm breasts were pressed to his chest, and he touched them through the fabric. She wriggled and moaned, and when he touched her nipples, she gasped with pleasure. Ethan held her buttocks and in one swift move was on top of her. Her mass of long hair covered the pillow and created a golden halo around her face. He lifted her top, and she helped him take it off to give him a full view of her magnificent firm breasts. He gazed at them in amazement and then held each one in his hand and rained them with little kisses.

Sarah looked serene and composed. Her lips were parted, and her eyes followed each of his movements with wonder. She was amazed at her body's reactions to Ethan's physical proximity and touch. She had often played with Guy, and they had even gone the whole way and had some kind of sex. But she had never experienced such intense feelings. He took one nipple in his mouth and started sucking it. His hands molded her breasts and pressed them to his face, which sent tinkling sensations to her brain. Sarah moaned and caressed his face and dug her fingers into his shoulders. She was aware of his weight over her and felt how her lower parts were craving his touch. She experienced rhythmic tremors running along her body, and her loins were getting wet. His erect penis was pressing into her, and she noticed how instinctively her thighs were parting to accommodate him.

Ethan was aware of what was happening with her, and he gave a deep moan and caught her mouth with a fierce kiss once again. He was a man obsessed. He left her mouth, caught her nipples, and gave them little bites. Soon his head went down to her navel, and he kissed and licked her lower abdomen. Sarah became more excited, and her hands caught his head, wondering where he was going to. He was close to her core, and she welcomed his experienced hands and mouth. He gradually lowered her panties while he was still looking into her beautiful eyes and seeking her approval.

Since he first met Sarah, Ethan couldn't get rid of the unique sensation that she was much more mature in many ways than her age. She was independent in her daily life, accustomed to making her own decisions, and quite versed with dealing with the adult world. However, what amazed him most now was the fact that she was natural and guileless when it came to her exceptional beauty and sex appeal. She truly enjoyed her sensuality, and unlike most young women he had known, she didn't pretend or actually experience any shame or fear. She had a free spirit and welcomed his intense interest in her with joy.

Sarah looked at his questioning eyes with swollen lips, and a consenting smile lit her face. She passed her tongue over her lips, and he felt how his heart had missed a beat. He bent his face into her warm and welcoming femininity. His hands exposed a luscious clump of chestnut pubic hair, and he covered it with kisses. He continued sending short glimpses toward her face while parting the hair. It was obvious that she was excited and enjoying his touch, and when he got closer to the swollen lips of her vagina, he began blowing warm air on them. His deft fingers gently parted the lips, and his hot tongue licked them and sent excruciating sensations into her brain. She didn't ease her hold on his shoulders, and her fingers dug into them with growing intensity. Her pelvis lifted itself of its own accord, and she gasped for air.

Ethan was relieved to realize she was not intact, and he didn't have to be the one to violate her virginity. He lifted his face and reached for her lips, which welcomed him and returned his kisses. He let her tongue dance with his for a while and then returned to the promising wealth between her thighs. He slowly increased his pressure on the lips, and his tongue seemed to have a life of its own. Her vagina was soaking wet with her special, perfumed liquid, and he seemed to savor her total response to his needs. He looked at her and was greatly pleased. Her eyes were smoldering, and her body was wriggling under his expert touches. Sarah moaned and called his name but never let go of him. She lifted her head and rained little kisses all over his head and chest and thus showed her approval of what he was doing to her body.

Time did not exist for both of them. Ethan was determined to make her reach her peak and release some of the tension from her body. He was painfully aware of his own needs but knew he would have to wait for another opportunity. He wanted to pleasure Sarah first and make her pass the threshold of intimacy between them before he could fully consummate full sexual intercourse with her. She was too precious for him, and he wanted her body to remember his imprint on it.

Sarah felt she was going to explode with all these new sensations her body was experiencing and the wealth of her own needs. She craved his little bites and wanted more of him inside her. He seemed to be tuned into her needs. His fingers found their way into her molten honey, and they ran havoc in her body and brain. Her skin tingled, and her breathing became heavier. She wanted to scream with pleasure and pushed his head even deeper into her pelvis while she sought relief, but he didn't relent. He went on exploring her core with the tip of his tongue and fingers, which reached her most hidden depths, and then she couldn't hold it anymore.

She exploded with endless bursts of molten lava that his probing tongue and fingers had created in her, and strong spasms convulsed her body. She gasped for air. After a long thrust of her pelvis the spasms subsided, and she fell back onto the bed with a satisfied sigh.

Ethan looked at her in wonder. He had never experienced such a feat with any of the women he had been with, and although he had not answered his own needs, he was greatly satisfied with the serene pleasure he saw on Sarah's face. He subliminally perceived that it was her first proper orgasm and was pleased to see the elusive change from a young girl into a woman take root in her eyes and demure. She passed her hands over his face and hair and smiled happily.

"Thank you. It was my first," she said, and after a short pause she continued, "My best." Although she spoke quietly, Ethan could detect Sarah's good old self surfacing, and he was happy. She was an amazing young woman, and he knew he had just experienced something rare and worth cherishing.

"You are welcome, sweetheart. I am happy I could cater for your needs, my lady."

She chuckled, but there was a serious concern in her eyes. "what about you? It wasn't all that good for you, was it?"

"It is all right. Don't worry about it. I wanted to pleasure you first because I think you are the most incredible person I know. As for my pleasure, well, I will think of something suitable." He looked at her naked body and marveled at her young, lovely figure, her mass of deep honey-colored hair and her red lips, which were still swollen and inviting. She smiled and pulled him down to kiss him. But before he bent over her, Ethan covered her with the bed sheet and tucked it around her.

"We'd better get up and have some breakfast. We have a long drive home today." He paused for a moment and searched her face. "I have also promised to stop at Robin's archeological dig to take some papers to the States." She didn't say anything, just got up and walked to the bathroom. She wasn't embarrassed or self-conscious about her nakedness, and he simply adored her.

After they showered and packed, they got down to a nearly empty dining room. However, the young waiter's pimpled face lit up when he saw Sarah, and they were quickly served a full, nourishing breakfast. They were both ravenous and in need of replenishing their energies.

Sarah looked relaxed and happy, and in no way did she display any sign of what she had gone through during the night and early morning. Ethan found it as hard as before to reconcile her behavior with the fact that she was only eighteen.

Chapter 10

The drive to Robin's archeological site was pleasant, and they talked about Ethan's plans and forthcoming return to the States. Sarah was cool about it. She asked about his work with his father and his plans to expand the business and his interest in building bridges, but she did not refer to his imminent flight back to the States.

Robin was nowhere to be seen when they arrived, so they walked around the site and talked to the many volunteers who were happy to share their new, hard-gained knowledge with them. And then suddenly Robin arrived. Sarah was amazed at the transformation in him. He looked urban and incongruous with a dark suit and trimmed beard and hair. He welcomed them cordially and, somehow clumsily, excused his new looks with the need to meet the local authorities on the matter of increasing the size of the site. Sarah could see Ethan's hidden smile behind his dark glasses, but they both refrained from any comments. She went forward and kissed Robin on his cheeks and sensed how his body relaxed.

They had lunch in a nearby village, and Sarah appreciated the professor's wit and wide knowledge in areas of ancient art or local politics. On their drive home, Ethan later asked her, "Did I tell you that Professor Robin Ford is a very talented violinist too and could have joined any major philharmonic orchestra? However, he preferred academic life and archeology, and maybe that is probably the main reason why his two marriages failed." Sarah suddenly recalled the one moment when she saw Robin looking at her and Ethan, and it seemed as if he had uncannily perceived the change in their relations, although he didn't comment on it in any way.

The drive home passed very quickly, and they were both too tired and preoccupied in their own thoughts to have a proper conversation. It was strange to be back home after just a few days and feel so different. She felt a little out of sorts because although everything at home was the same, Sarah felt she had changed. The pain of losing Guy and the absence of her father were as acute as before, but she could contain it. She became a bit agitated with the many messages and notes that were left for her, but she decided to keep her silence for a while. She called David and was told that her father had decided after all to return earlier and that they could expect him during the weekend. Ethan had left for the city after a quick shower and change of clothes.

It was dusk, and the western horizon was magnificent with the flaming colors of the setting sun descending into the shimmering silver expanse of the sea.

Sarah felt a great need to be in the familiar ambiance of the sea, so she went for a swim. The ancient rock was warm, and it was wonderful to lie down and just soak in the warmth of the stone with the last rays of sun. She thought of Ethan and how he might join her on the stone, but it was already dark when she returned home and began preparing supper with the products they had bought on their return.

Ethan returned quite late, and from the look on his face Sarah knew he was upset and preoccupied with something; however, she refrained from saying anything. His face lit up when he saw her in her short, pretty summer dress and kissed her lightly on her nose. "Hello, beautiful, everything okay?"

She gave him a side glance and offered him a bottle of cold beer.

They had their supper on the porch, and Sarah told him her father was returning a few days early, which was wonderful news. She suggested a walk on the beach, and Ethan seemed happy to go out.

He wore his cut jeans with a T-shirt, and they walked bare feet along the seashore. At some point he caught her hands and brought them to his lips and kissed them. The light breeze scattered her hair around her face, and he weaved his fingers into their mass and held her close.

"For the life of me I don't know anybody in the world like you." His eyes kept searching her lustrous dark gray eyes for a clue, but he was at a loss for an answer. "You are smart, beautiful, and wise. You are more poised than women twice your age. Where did you come from into my life?"

He spoke slowly and quietly as if he were talking to himself. "You know you have bewitched me in just few days, and I am at a loss." He held her face close to his chest and whispered in her ears, "I have to leave you tomorrow and fly back. My father is in some predicament, and he needs me beside him." He gave a deep sigh and continued, "How am I going to leave you?"

Sarah lifted her head slowly and gazed into his anguished eyes. She kissed them both, took his hand, and turned toward home.

After she locked the doors, she took him into her room and left the windows wide open for the fresh evening breeze.

"I love the sound and smell of the sea, and I hope you don't mind me leaving it open," she said and began pulling off his T-shirt. "I want to see the whole of you. Is it okay with you?" He was in a daze. She stood in front of him with only her flimsy panties and beckoned him to come closer.

Sarah was magnificent. The two firm globs of her breasts, her golden skin which glowed from the sun, and the patch of chestnut hair between her thighs elicited some dangerous sensations in his loins. He felt how his manhood was trying to find release from its confinement and felt embarrassed. He gasped when she touched the bulge in his jeans and opened the zipper. Her mere touch set his whole body on fire. Her hands slipped his boxers down his thighs, and there his gloriously erect penis was. She looked at it with wonder and took it in her hands. "You are so beautiful and exciting." She paused and then continued seriously, "I see you must be excited to see me too." She smiled and then continued more seriously, "I want to make love with you."

For a moment he felt like an adolescent before his first sexual encounter, but the tension and pressure in his loins were too much to bear. He lifted her up in the air and laid her on the bed and lay beside her. "Are you sure?" he asked with sincere concern in his voice.

She nodded her head. "I am on the pill, so you don't have to worry." She never ceased to amaze him.

Sarah seemed to have entered into a candy shop. She touched and caressed every part of his body. She kissed his eyes, his lips, and his eyebrows. She bit his earlobes lightly and then went to his arms and chest. She kept murmuring to herself, "You are so handsome, so strong, and so sexy." Her long massive curls engulfed his face, and the long strands got into his mouth and tickled his skin. Her thighs were stretched on top of his, and she didn't let him wriggle away from under her weight. "Now it is my turn, so keep still and suffer." He chuckled, and she gave his lips a small bite.

Sarah was methodical and focused in her endeavor to please them both. From time to time, she passed her tongue over her lips like a child expecting a big treat. She had one hand in his thick hair, and the other explored his skin and limbs. His erect nipples seemed to fascinate her, and she pinched and licked them lightly with the tip of her tongue. Ethan followed her movement with awe and could feel how each touch stoked the fire of desire in him and rendered him powerless.

Sarah gradually turned her attention to his lower part while she still grinded into his erection with her pelvis. Her supple fingers lifted each of his tight buttocks and pressed them to her chest. She lifted her eyes to his, and there was deep desire with a glimpse of humor in them. She was enjoying herself. She parted his thighs, and her fingers traveled to their inner flesh. His whole body was toned and lean. He was a lovely specimen of manhood. She licked the inner skin of his thighs and ignored his desperate need for her to touch the core of his desire.

At last Sarah diverted her attention to his prominent erection and swollen balls. First she blew hot air over them, and then she used the tip of her tongue to lick the folds of his shaft. Her hands began weighing and molding his balls. Ethan started moaning and twisting his body, seeking greater release from the mass of sensations and desires that flooded him. She looked at him in warning, but it was too late. He grabbed both her arms, and in one swift move he turned them around. Now she was below him and at his mercy as he pinned both her hands above her head and ravished her mouth. He was a man obsessed and at the end of his tether. He wanted release for all the explosion of desires and needs that had been building up in him for so many days and nights. He wanted to be inside her where he had found her depth of molten fire before. He wanted her to experience the same desperate need for him as he had for her.

Sarah lay content to let him take over. All her senses were finely tuned to receive him into her. She desperately desired him but let him lead the way. After her experience the morning near the lake, her body craved his touch and a mutual fulfillment. She recalled how Ethan made her reach her first climax and how exquisite it felt. He made her come again and again, and at the end her body simply collapsed. She knew it was a once-in-a-lifetime experience that she would never forget; but now it was different. She wanted Ethan to experience it together with her, and he seemed to share her need. He parted her thighs and at once devoured her mouth.

He lifted her breasts and sucked each nipple as if they were candies while Sarah's hands reached his erect penis and bulging balls. Ethan moaned. He tried to reach her center with his mouth to pleasure her again, but Sarah's hands were a buffer, and she directed his trembling hot shaft toward her craving vagina.

The first instant Ethan penetrated her proved to be explosive, and each second her sensations heightened to such degree that she felt like screaming. Then he began his thrusts into her pelvis while his penis reached unknown depths. His fingers joined the inner dance when they pinched and twisted her clitoris and center of pleasure. Sarah moaned and cried his name and held him tightly to her own convulsing body with her strong thighs and legs. Ethan was in frenzy. He sought relief yet wished to savor the act as long as possible.

Sarah caught his mouth and sucked his lips while her pelvis and legs joined him in a synchronized dance culminating in a mutual burst of spasms along their twined bodies. He felt how the molten stream that had gathered in his loins since he first laid eyes on Sarah flowed into her equally hot cavity and blended into a wonderful sense of relief and tenderness. He wondered about the last time he had felt in such harmony with himself and when he would have that feeling again.

A symphony of sensations and yearnings washed all over him, and he embraced her to himself and buried his face in the perfumed cascade of her hair.

Chapter 11

Ethan had to leave early the next morning for his flight home, and both Sarah and Ethan were sated and depleted from a night of wondrous pleasures and sensations. Once his body had released its first pent-up need for her and his continuous wish to touch her and contain her magic, he lay quietly and wondered why it had been so different from any other climaxes he had experienced before.

He realized that though Sarah seemed to be a novice in sexual experience, she possessed a unique blend of curiosity, generosity, and capacity to enjoy the pleasures of her body. She was curious to experience every nuance and move Ethan chose to share with her. She was blissfully unaware of the beauty of her young and attractive body and marveled at the mastery and expertise of Ethan. She was amazed to see him riveted to her every limb and facial expressions. She wanted to please him as much as he pleased her.

Sarah was in full accord with her body and sexuality, and Ethan was eternally grateful for it. She kissed and sucked his lips; caressed his torso from the crown of his hair to his toes, and all the time moved her full breasts along his body. It took Ethan short moments to reach full erection again, and Sarah was there, fondling and squeezing his erection between her breasts. Ethan spread her thighs and sucked her flowing nectar with his mouth. He was relentless with his fingers, probing her inner sanctum and teasing her clitoris into frenzy. She wriggled and twisted her body, which increased his desire for her. He could feel her coming and coming, and she lifted her pelvis and inserted his shaft into her craving depth.

This time it was less frantic, and Ethan carried her further and further into new realms of pleasure. He wanted to prolong the sensation to its edge and continued with his deep thrusts into her. She called his name and begged him to stop, yet he thrust his tongue into her mouth and filled it with his hot breath. Sarah felt how both his tongue and penis created the most wonderful sensations and sense of release in her body, and it felt as if she was emitting fireworks and taking Ethan with her.

She lay her head on his breast and immediately fell asleep. Ethan's body was unusually tranquil and sated, but his mind was in a mush. He looked upon Sarah's full lips and bent down to kiss them. She smiled in her sleep and cuddled into him. Suddenly he was terrified of the thought that he might not be with her again like this, and he wanted to cry. His hands fondled her breasts, and he buried his face in her hair.

He must have fallen asleep, for it took him few minutes to pass from oblivion to the realization that he was in full erection again. Sarah was holding the tip of his erection in her mouth. She was sprawled over him, and her hair was spread around his genitals as she was looking at him with sparkling eyes. "I thought you might like it. I know I do when you do it to me." He was speechless. She had this impish smile that said, "I can be as good as you," and he didn't doubt her.

She gently inserted his moist shaft into her vagina. He felt an electrical jolt along his spine. Slowly she held both her breasts and carried them to his mouth. Her body stretched on top of his, and he felt how his erection came to life and throbbed with a will of its own. He caught her breasts and showered them with kisses. It was so splendid he felt like crying or like evaporating into one entity and containing her forever.

Gradually he became aware of the first signs of dawn and the early rays of sun penetrating through the open window, tainting the long chestnut strands of her hair with gold and forming a special lighted tent around their heads. Ethan wanted to tell her how wondrous and unique this whole encounter with her had been for him and how enchanted and awed he was with her, but he also knew he had no right to burden her with anything but his silent gratitude for being what she was.

They made love once again, and this time it was done leisurely and tenderly, as each knew it was the last time and was intent on pleasing the other.

Chapter 12
Older Sarah

I must admit that the recollection of those past events arouses a mixture of feelings, memories, and reflections. It is one thing to experience at present similar erotic and sensual feelings I had felt more than half a century before, but what baffles me is the intensity and clarity of the experience now.

I recall how sad and intense and yet sweet and wondrous it was to be eighteen and experience one of the most basic and most profound physical experiences in life in close proximity to the death of my first love. I often wondered how lucky I was to have had Ethan next to me just when Guy died. I was blessed to have had Ethan to initiate me through my first full sexual experience and thus mark my attitude and enjoyment of all erotic intercourse between men and women for life.

The next time I heard from Ethan was when he called me to congratulate me on my wedding. I was totally in love with Michael, my future husband, yet I was happy to speak with Ethan. He always had a special place in my heart.

Ethan ended his words of congratulations with a request from me to pursue my own happiness and not let life change me. We met again many years later. Well, I don't think I have changed much since that week with Ethan. I am still eighteen years old.

My father once mentioned to me that Ethan had actually gotten married, but it didn't last long. He had one son and spent much time in the Far East, where he built bridges and climbed the mountains.

On reflection I know that Ethan was an important milestone in the formation of my adult life, and in fact, he affected the course of how I would approach sex. I believe every young woman should have her first sexual encounter with an experienced and mature lover like Ethan.

However, this last encounter with a spirited entity and my body's reaction to it astonishes and bewilders me. I still engage from time to time in sexual intercourse, and though it is fine for both of us and provides us pleasure and some form of release, it is not like how it used to be.

The early morning ethereal apparition is a strong reminder of what I still remember about how it had been and what it should be like.

In my mind I decided to call him Ariel. I don't know whether it was a result of my acquaintance with Ariel from Shakespeare's *The Tempest* because it had that airy, ethereal, and amorphous aura about it. I can never determine in my mind whether it was a dream, a figment of my imagination, or something related to my age and its need for rejuvenation and sexual excitement. After the first several encounters with its presence in the vicinity of my bedroom at the very early hours of the morning, I am used to his presence. He rarely appears in the other hours of the day, and he best communicates with me while I am half asleep and my body is relaxed and languid.

I remember my parents being very handsome and loving people. I still recall my father kissing and embracing my mother openly in front of my brother and me. My mother had a lovely voice, and she would often serenade him on festive occasions. It broke my heart when she died so young and left my warm and loving father a widower. It took him many years to begin dating again, and only after I had left home for university did he bring Ruth home. She was a wonderful mate for him, and my brother and I loved her very much because she also made our father happy.

My whole life I have never refrained from publicly showing affection in different forms and in a variety of situations. My brother, David, openly kisses and hugs his wife along with his two young children and grandchildren, and in return they all shower much love and affection on my father and me. As time goes by, I find it easy to be affectionate and show it in public toward my family and friends. It never embarrasses me. So when I feel Ariel pat my hair or touch my breasts in passing around the house, I can detect his affection and caring nature.

I love to touch and feel those who are dear and special to me. I don't mean to say that I touch strangers and people in general.

No, only those I love and care for. It is so much easier to convey feelings of joy and well-being just by touching and without saying anything. A smile and a wink can also achieve the same result, but by lightly touching the other, especially a lover or a husband, the rewards and pleasures are multiplied. I am sorry I get carried away with my thoughts, but alas, I am not a spring chicken anymore.

On the days Ariel visits me, I am in a constant high. Apart from the random touching and whispering hot nothings into my ear, he takes off years of life's weight from different folds of my body. After each visit I can feel my skin smoother, my arms and thighs lighter, and the passage into an aura of bliss lingers with me for long hours. Ariel does not only lead me to speak of sexual fulfillment, but he also helps me review my past life and be at peace with the present.

In the course of my life I have often observed how humans and animals behave sexually and find this strong and primal need natural and blissful. However, I could never abide with its extreme manifestations in humans. I have never been able to condone or accept the compulsive drive to consummate a sexual act by force ... or as an act of punishment on somebody else. I simply don't. I am neither naïve nor innocent when it comes to deviations in human nature or conduct; however, I can never identify with or forgive cruel or beastly sexual behavior, which debases and hurts in any form or under any circumstances.

I realize I don't have any psychological qualifications to analyze or explain the compulsions that drive people to act cruelly and without consent of the other when engaged in sexual behavior. I do, however, know I abhor and resent any attempt to justify it in normal human discourse.

I know that when a man is compelled to abuse the sexual act, he is more of a mindless beast than a human.

The morning came into my room through the window cracks, and I became partially awake, trying to recall my dreams. I remember swimming in the sea near my father's home where I live now, and I remember somebody swimming next to me in the dark. He was strong and powerful and instilled quiet confidence in me, but he kept following me and not leading the way. I couldn't see his face, but he surely was encouraging me to continue and reach the rock before him.

I wonder who it is. Suddenly I am aware of Ariel, who gently transfers me into another realm of dreams mixed with reality.

Chapter 13
Young Sarah

Michael came into her life when she was about twenty four years old and toward the end of her postgraduate studies at the university. She was majoring in biology and took Greek philosophy as a minor. She intended to go for her PhD the following year, while Michael was already finishing his doctorate in math and computers and dabbling with some ancient philosophy. He told her once that whatever mathematics and geometry there was to learn was born with the two ancient Greek giants Archimedes and Pythagoras. He was fascinated with their superior ability to conceive abstract mathematical notions without the accumulated knowledge of modern science.

Sarah and Michael had occasionally noticed each other before they actually met in some student events or bars around town, but they had never spoken or dated each other. They didn't move in the same social circles. He was three years older and had a lot of beautiful young women around him. He looked like a hunk with his broad shoulders and towering height; however, his gold-rimmed glasses were sometimes a giveaway and hid a more sensitive nature. He was considered a brilliant mathematician and very much sought after by emerging new computer companies that were looking for young talents.

As Sarah was not dating anybody at the time, she did notice his presence amidst the regular body of mostly female students who ogled him and tried to sit next to him during ancient philosophy lectures.

Professor Sharpstein was very popular among his students. His lecture halls were packed not only because of Socrates or Plato's observations on human nature and morals but also because of his own sharp and very often poignant remarks about the nature of all students ancient or modern. He especially liked to speak to some imaginary female students and ask them whether they had accomplished at the university what they had come to do, namely catch a husband. Or he would ask them how much they had drunk or what the subjects of discussion were in the latest *modern symposiums* they had participated in. Invariably his remarks were accompanied with bursts of laughter mixed with feelings of discomfort among some students who somehow considered his remarks directed at them.

Sarah found him very erudite, interesting, amusing, and slightly offensive too, but she refrained from making any remarks, which the professor greatly encouraged.

Professor Sharpstein was a distant cousin of her late mother, so she had known him through family gatherings, and her father was on friendly terms with him; however, she never hinted or said anything to that effect to him or others. Once, however, during one of his tirades with a female student, he turned to her personally and asked her, "Sarah, why, in your opinion, weren't there many women students and philosophers among Greek scholars, and would you possibly consider the cause to be the inferior minds of women why Socrates, Plato, and others refrained from encouraging women in general to participate in their schools?"

Sarah was as surprised as everybody else in the audience from his direct question to her. The fact that he mentioned her name, singled her out, and showed some personal interest in her, which she viewed with some dismay, surprised the others. She was sitting by herself in the last row near the wall and could see how nearly everybody was looking at her with interest, including Michael, who had now turned his head with anticipation to see how she would react.

Sarah felt how her face was flushed with red, but with some effort she ignored all the expectant faces in the room and looked directly at Professor Sharpstein. "I suppose that one could find many reasons inherent in the political and social system of the time in Athens and the ancient world as responsible for this bizarre state of affairs, but if I were to explain it more to the point, I would use the means of an analogy. Just consider it even took God to make a draft before he created his masterpiece, namely a woman. So it is understandable, and we can forgive Socrates, Plato, and the others if they had not yet reached that stage of recognizing a superior species." She paused for a minute and continued, "Anyway, what would have happened to all the universities around the world now and mainly to the philosophy departments if women didn't have free access to academic studies?"

All the students were stunned from her sharp and half-mocking answer. Professor Sharpstein's small piercing eyes narrowed, and he had a certain smile at the corner of his mouth. He seemed quite pleased with her quick retort and took his time before he answered her. "I concede there is some merit to your argument; however, I beg to differ on behalf of Socrates and his friends to your use of a Jewish or Christian deity in the Pantheon of Zeus, Apollo, and Athens. And as to you women folk, I would not forfeit your place in my lectures for all the tea in China." Everybody breathed a sigh of relief, and the room exploded with applause. She smiled back at the professor and acknowledged the fact that they knew each other and that the whole interlude was only in jest.

Sarah began to relax and felt how the Professor's answer defused the tension in the room and gave her some time to gather herself. The professor waited for few moments and then continued in a more sober tone, "I hope you would all have valid arguments for your end-of-term test questions."

Chapter 14

After the lecture the students began to disperse, and she saw Michael approaching her, his blue eyes behind the gold-rimmed glasses never leaving her face. She knew who he was while he introduced himself. "I am Michael Goren. Would you care to have coffee with me now?" He was nearly two meter tall, and it was clear from his gait that he exercised regularly. What struck her immediately was the contrast between his very fair skin and his dark hair and eyebrows. She noticed he had the most piercing blue eyes and he needed a haircut.

In the past she had been slightly intrigued by his presence in Professor Sharpstein's lectures, and now she smiled at him. "I would love to," she said. They sat in the main cafeteria, and many students came to congratulate her on her answer to the obnoxious professor and patted her on her shoulders. She felt slightly embarrassed but kept up the light banter.

Michael only asked her if she knew the professor personally, and she had to tell him about her distant family ties with him.

"The last time I met him was at my brother's wedding four years ago. He is my late mother's cousin, and my father likes him very much. I think they studied together at some time. I didn't think he recognized me from that distance, but I should have trusted him to know everything about his students. My father says he is very shrewd and focused."

"I must say I was surprised when he singled you out with that tricky question in the lecture. How did you feel about it?" Michael was serious, and she didn't hesitate to tell him her real opinion.

"I was surprised at first but not offended. The question was a little provocative but very much in line with his general approach to women. He is more comfortable discussing philosophical, political, and business matter with men than with women. In his opinion we are very good for decoration. However, he knows my opinion in these matters from the past. My father had once hinted to me that he was very much interested in my mother, but she had rejected him on similar grounds and married my father, who is just the opposite." She went quiet and looked at him questionably. "I am sorry, but you asked for it. And what's more, now you know very essential information about me."

Michael continued looking at her for few minutes and seemed to be considering her words seriously and then he said, "I have to return to work now, but would you have dinner with me some time?" His reaction was unexpected, and Sarah looked at him with surprise; however, he continued, "If you are not dating anybody at the moment, I suggest just dinner and talk. Is it okay with you?"

Sarah smiled, and finding his direct style of talk appealing, she didn't hesitate. "I would like to have dinner with you but only toward the end of the weekend."

"Done. I will call you." He didn't ask for her phone number or address. Sarah guessed a bright young man like Michael would surely have ways to get information about her. He got up from the table and seemed to be preoccupied with something. "I am happy to have met you. I will see you soon." He turned and walked away.

He called late on Thursday night, and Sara realized it was a long-distance call. "I am abroad, and I won't make it home this weekend. Do you mind if I take a rain check? I will call you after I return." He paused for a moment and continued, "Sarah, are you with me?"

She smiled to herself. She knew many people found her habit of just listening to the other and not interfering in the middle until they finished speaking quite disconcerting. "Yes, I am here. It is perfectly fine with me."

"Did I put you out in any way?"

"No, I am quite fine, and it would be lovely to see you after you return." She didn't ask him where he was or why he had gone away. He must have had his own reasons, and anyway, she had no hold on his time and didn't mind at all.

Her days and nights were filled with studies, tests, papers, the gym, and going out with friends. Her father had built her a spacious apartment unit attached to the main house, so she could still enjoy the beach and her family whenever she had time.

Chapter 15

It was Tuesday afternoon, her shortest day at university. She decided to go swimming, and when she came out of the water and saw a figure of a man on the porch of her father's house, it gave her a strange feeling of déjà vu. However, it was Michael.

The first thing that came to her mind was the fact she was lucky to be wearing her swimsuit unlike what she normally used to do when she was on her own. The second thought that crossed her mind was *Ethan*. She wrapped herself with her beach towel and walked slowly toward him. The memory of Ethan just washed over her, and she could see some of the similarities and differences between the two men.

Michael was tall and on the fair side. His dark hair was straight and parted in the middle, and some hair always fell over his face. He had a high forehead, and she knew his eyes were piercing blue behind his sunglasses. He was more light and catlike on his feet than most men she knew, and there was a unique quiet about him. He looked tired and unkempt, and Sarah was happy to see him. It gave her heart a strange jolt to see him on the same spot where Ethan had first met her, but she welcomed his unannounced presence and smiled at him.

"Good to see you." There was no point asking him how he had found her home. Somehow she knew it was part of being Michael.

"I am happy to be here. I knew from your schedule this was your short day, so I decided to take a risk and come here directly from the airport." He stood there and seemed to be lost a little. "I hope you don't mind."

Michael looked as if he was mesmerized by her. He had been standing there for quite a while and watching her swim from the rock to the beach. She was an Amazon. Her tall, lean body was encased in a full swimsuit that extenuated her lushes figure and stocked his imagination. He knew she had a nice figure, but seeing her now—her sleek, tanned skin dripping with water, her long hair pulled back from her face, and those full and beautiful lips—just beckoned him to touch her.

"Do you swim a lot?" it was an inane question, but he couldn't help staring at her.

"Yes, I do. I am glad you came. You must be tired, so—" She took his hand in hers and walked into her own house and continued, "We'd better get in before Ruth, my father's wife, wonders what is going on."

Michael had flown nonstop for nearly twenty hours throughout the United States and back home. He was exhausted and needed sleep desperately, yet on the flight home he had this urge to see Sarah before he met up with his father and reported about his meetings or went to sleep. He had her in the back of his mind the whole time. He didn't dwell on the why and where of it; her face was imprinted in his memory, and she was just there. He knew he would have to deal with it some time. Now he felt unusually happy to be with her, and that was enough for him.

Sarah offered him some iced tea and excused herself to take a shower. She asked him to help himself to anything else he needed and disappeared into the back of the house. The cool and simply furnished drawing room was pleasant. It was part of an open kitchen and extended into a wooden porch looking onto the sea with its own comfortable wicker chairs and a glass table. The house was shaded from outside by a line of poplar trees and a mixture of shrubs and cacti. The drawing room was full of plants, and the walls were covered with works of contemporary artists. The drawing room was an extension of the kitchen area with a small dining table and chairs. An old, green leather sofa bordered the sitting area with a reclining chair, two comfortable-looking armchairs and a wooden coffee table in the middle.

There was the sound of quiet jazz music coming out from somewhere, and Michael felt how his body was relaxing when he sagged into the inviting armchair with a cool glass of iced tea in his hand. He gazed into the shining blue expense of the sea and closed his eyes.

Sarah walked with bare feet into the room, wearing short jeans and a white T-shirt. Her long hair was still wet in a ponytail. Michael was asleep, and she wondered why it felt so natural to have him in her home. She examined his face, and though he was tired and unshaved, he looked virile and appealing. She went out into the porch and stood watching her favorite spot in the sea. The sun, a huge golden globe, was quickly approaching the horizon, and the shimmering surface of the sea was rippling with small waves. She could see her favorite rock since childhood, where she had spent many restful hours either alone or with various friends, and yes, there was Ethan too and the painful memory of Guy. She snapped out of her reveries and returned to the room.

Michael was standing there and watching her. "I am sorry to have crashed in on you. I should go home." He was embarrassed and ill at ease, but Sarah knew she was happy to see him and offered a light supper on the porch. Michael fell into step with her and helped lay the table with dishes and glasses. Sarah made a simple salad, and he volunteered to prepare his "mean" omelet. They were both surprised at the ease and comfort they felt with each other. Michael couldn't believe it was only the second time he had met her. He had already fallen asleep in her armchair, and here he was making an omelet and telling her about his trip and why he liked the United States.

Sarah had this uniquely ingrained quality to listen, and when Michael started telling her about his new invention in the computerized electronic field he and his father had been working on, she listened attentively. She was truly fascinated with his deep voice but mainly with his passion and commitment to his dreams and visions. He was involved with his work and pulled Sarah into his realm. Michael was fascinated with what could be done with the combination of electronics and computers. Though he was much involved in the writing of new programs for his thesis, his mind was engaged in using both these fields for commercial purposes.

His parents lived in the next town, and he had one younger brother who lived in London. He was a musician and already played with the Young Philharmonic Orchestra. Michael seemed to be fond of his younger brother and took every opportunity to visit him. "He is a great guy, and he knows his London well. I am sure you would both like each other." Sarah was surprised but said nothing to disturb him from telling his story.

His father had an electronic company, and his mother was a nurse. He lived on his own and loved extreme sport. He suddenly stopped and said, "Ah, I hope you don't mind, but I took the liberty of compensating you for the ruined weekend." He went to his case and produced a small, beautifully wrapped green package. It was a small but beautiful bottle of Miss Dior perfume.

Sarah was shocked. It was her favorite perfume, and she had inherited it from her late mother. "How did you know this was my perfume?" she asked in astonishment.

"I remember smelling it on you in the cafeteria and asked the saleslady in the duty free in the airport to let me smell all the leading perfumes there were. The third one was this. It smells good on you.'

Sarah liked this fragrance most because of its subtle perfume, its unique blend of the essence of fresh flowers and exotic fruit and herbs. She remembered her mother wearing mostly this fragrance. "Thanks. You couldn't have given me anything better." Here she blushed a little and said, "Although I don't think I deserve it."

"I think you do," he said so solemnly that she felt the tension in his voice.

"Come, let us have some coffee."

"I would love to have some coffee, but after it I must leave for home. I would love to call my parents and then fall asleep in the shower." He smiled with his self-effacing humor, and Sarah liked him the more.

Michael left after a short while, and as he got into his yellow mini minor, he said, "We still have a date this weekend, okay?"

Sarah nodded and felt happy.

Chapter 16

He called on her on Friday evening. He looked quite debonair in his new pair of jeans, a light blue shirt, and a dark blue blazer. He was combed and shaved and looked quite fresh.

"You look as if you have managed to overcome your jet lag and catch up on your sleep," she said, and he smiled.

"You look good too."

She was wearing a white cotton dress with a small bolero in green. She looked wonderful. Her mass of honey-streaked chestnut hair was sprayed on her bare shoulders, and he felt an urge to put his fingers in it and feel its texture and smell it.

Michael could discern the lingering scent of the Dior on her and gave her a peck on her cheek. "I wanted to take my parents' family car, but I thought if they wished to go out, it would be rather hard for my mother to crawl into my Mini. I hope you don't mind it."

"Of course not, I love Mini cars, and I have one red one myself. But it's not as new as yours."

Michael took her to a small bistro in the old city, and they sat at a secluded corner table where they could talk quietly and peacefully. Michael was a very attentive partner. He asked about her studies, her travels around the world, and her aspirations. None of the questions was intrusive, yet while he was telling her about his own life, he inquired whether she had done the same or had visited similar places. Sarah was impressed with his accomplishments.

At the age of twenty-seven he had nearly finished his PhD in applied mathematics and owned his own small computer company. He employed about ten young computer engineering students, and his father oversaw the work when he was absent abroad or engaged in his studies. He also tutored a postgraduate class in math at the university.

"To tell you the truth, one of the courses I enjoy most in my studies is Professor Sharpstein's. He is really sharp and even funny at times, but I can see you don't always find him amusing."

Sarah was pleased that he had raised the topic of bigotry and gender discrimination among the majority of male faculty members. Although she had never faced any direct discrimination directed toward her, she was fully aware of the situation and resented it. "I am not much worried or concerned with Professor Sharpstein's remarks about the university being the matching grounds for 'would-be married female students.' He is old school, and he acts the same in real life; however, the fact that many younger lecturers raise eyebrows when they find women students in their science classes really irritates me. For example, the head of my biology department asked me when she interviewed me for work in the university laboratory whether I was sure I didn't want to study sociology or art instead of biology and chemistry. It was much easier than the sciences."

Michael could feel she was quite irked about the subject, and he sympathized with her. His mother was a feminist, and he grew up in a household that believed in and functioned on equality. "You have a sister in arms with my mother. She would gladly chew the professor for breakfast if he were to utter his remarks in her presence," he said with a smile.

"You can see why my mother preferred my father over him. What's more, my father is a darling and adored my mother," she said it with pride, but there was a whiff of sadness in her voice. "You would have loved my mother. She was beautiful both from outside and from inside. I still miss her every day."

The meal was wonderful, and they both enjoyed the fresh salad and succulent steaks they had ordered. He asked her if she would like to go to a discotheque where they could have a drink and listen to music too. Sarah was delighted. Although she didn't frequent discotheques, she loved dancing.

The music was soft rock and featured the Beatles, Elvis, and many other popular bands. They ordered their drinks and listened to the music. At one stage he dragged her onto the crowded dance floor and whirled her around. The vigorous rock and roll movements released a gate on a dam of pent-up energy in her. It had been months since she had gone dancing and drinking.

Michael was a good match for her. He was really tuned to the music and easily synchronized with her steps. The long string of fast music changed into a dreamy Latin tune, and Michael caught her in his arms and kept her close to his body. At first she joined him in a natural movement, but she suddenly became aware of his arm around her waist and the other resting on her shoulder. He was looking into her eyes with an enigmatic look in them. She remembered seeing him with glasses and wondered whether he wore them only for reading. They were deep blue, and she wasn't sure whether he was amused or worried.

"I love your hair. May I touch it?" he asked with awe, and Sarah was moved.

He was very strong and virile yet gentle and reserved at the same time. She put her head on his shoulder, and his fingers lightly touched the long strands of her hair. The music was wonderful, and Sarah felt how the drinks, the music, and Michael's proximity were lulling her into a dreamy state of mind. Her hand had crawled up his shoulder and onto his neck. She could feel him stiffen for a moment. Then his body sagged into hers, and he held her even more tightly than before.

Sarah felt relaxed and content in Michael's arms, and when the disc jockey began playing fast music again, she didn't feel like joining in. She was reluctant to detach herself from the warmth and support of Michael's body, so she indicated they leave for home. Michael also seemed to be ready to leave. He took her hand and walked toward his car. "I am going to be away for a week or so. I shall call you before I return." They were in the car, and there was a new intimacy between them. "I shall tell you all about it after I return."

She nodded and sank into her seat.

"Did you enjoy yourself?" There was genuine concern in his voice, and she smiled happily.

"It has been a long time since I drank and danced so much." She stretched her hand and touched his shoulder. "The whole evening was great. You are quite a good dancer. I don't know many guys who can dance so well and enjoy it as much as you."

He smiled and said, "You should thank my mother for it. She taught me and my brother how to dance from an early age. She told us that it was the best and easiest way to impress pretty girls. Well, now I see she was right."

She chuckled. "I am sure you have been using your dancing skills for many years and on many unsuspecting damsels." She smiled and continued, "Don't forget to thank your mother. She must be one foxy lady."

He leaned his head back on the seat and burst into peals of laughter. "Well, I will be sure to convey your comments to her when I see her next."

Michael walked her to her door and waited for her to turn on the light and get in. "Take care, and I'll be back." And just before he left, he gave a small peck on her lips and drove away. Sarah had not felt so excited and happy in a long time. She had dated quite a few guys in recent years, but none of them had left her with such a feeling of content and inner peace of mind. She didn't normally like to dwell on things and ponder about what would be or not be. She knew she liked Michael, and it was right to wait for him.

Chapter 17

As it happened, Sarah had to finish her thesis and begin her PhD in microbiology. Her subject was the unique methods of proliferation among fungi. She knew it was a vast subject, and she wanted to concentrate on its relevancy to humans. She had already discussed it with her professor, and he had agreed to tutor her.

From time to time during the week Sarah wondered what Michael was doing abroad, but she left the wondering for the time he returned.

It was midterm time, and Sarah was busy with her load of papers and lab work. She had been tutoring a class of freshmen too, and she hardly had much free time to fret or miss Michael. Once, she came across his name by chance in the cafeteria. She was having lunch when a group of students sat next to her and continued talking about this lucky genius who had come up with a very ingenious electronic application in communication. The mobile phone or handheld phone, as it was called, was already a gadget that intrigued and attracted a lot of attention all over the world, and after they had mentioned his name several times, Sarah realized they were talking about Michael.

Apparently he had come from a well-to-do family and had been working in his father's electronic firm since his youth. He had lived with his family for few years in Boston, where he had studied and worked at Bell Company at the same time. Sarah was amazed at the amount of information the guys knew about Michael and how much attention he had drawn. One guy said he had heard that Michael had written a patent on his invention and that once he sold it, he would make a fortune.

Sarah felt embarrassed and uncomfortable with all these revelations about Michael. She would rather hear them from Michael and not through a bunch of gossiping students. She got up and returned to her lab.

Michael called after a day and sounded tired yet jubilant at the same time. "I have some good news, but I will tell you about it once I get back home. However, I am going to be delayed for few more days." He took a short breath and asked, "Would you wait for me?"

She laughed and said, "I am not going anywhere, and yes, I'll be here."

"Good. I'm looking forward to seeing you." As he finished the call, Sarah thought she detected a moment of hesitation in his voice just before he put the phone down, but she let it pass.

It had not been long since Sarah first met Michael and began dating him, and deep down in her heart she knew he was the one she would like to know better and deepen their relationship. She could feel how she was attracted to him not only physically but mentally as well. They agreed on so many subjects like children, loyalty, and commitment to one's values at work and between people. Sarah loved discussing issues and problems in her own studies with her father and brother, and it pleased her to see how seriously Michael regarded each subject she brought up and how earnestly he listened to her opinions. She missed his immediate presence in town, the excitement she felt when he held her hand or leaned over to tell her something private.

It was early evening, and the weather was cold and windy. Sarah had just finished her last tutorial of the day, and she was on her way to her car. As she was locking her door, she saw him leaning on the wall near the elevators and studying her. He seemed to be pondering something serious; however, as he caught her eyes, his face lit up with a big smile, and he gave her a bear hug.

"I know you are exhausted, but you look lovely." He pulled her face away from him and studied her eyes. "Are you happy to see me?" He didn't wait for her answer and continued, "I wanted to see you before I went home." She smiled openly, and there was a twinkle in them.

"I am happy to see you, Michael Goren." She gave him a small kiss on his lips and took his hand. "Let's leave this building. Do you fancy eating anything? I haven't eaten anything all day, how about you?"

"Well, the jet leg confuses my biological clock, but I do not care what we are going to eat." They reached the street level and agreed to walk to the nearest sandwich bar down the street.

The bar was nearly empty, as it was too early for the night crowd and too late for the lunch crowd. They were happy to sit at a corner table and order some drinks. It seemed Michael was very eager to share with her his news, but they waited for their drinks before Michael began talking. Normally Sarah would order her favorite gin and tonic with ice and lemon, and he would order his scotch on the rock; however, this evening they both ordered beer.

As they were left alone, he began telling her about his "small" breakthrough and how he had managed to interest an international company in his invention. "You know I studied applied math and I deal with computers and electronics. It seems to me the world is facing a revolutionary change in the field of stationary and handheld telephones, and I mean to be involved in it." He took her hands in his, and there were sparkles in his eyes. "I have come up with some new software solutions that can help this process. The people of IBM are very keen on it, and they have signed a contract with my company to develop it with them here and in the States."

Michael was excited and keen to share his ideas and thoughts with her. Suddenly Sarah realized that Michael was very unique and important to her. She listened to his explanations and heard his unadulterated enthusiasm and was happy to have been singled out by him. He was young, bright, and fully committed to his dreams and vision. She was attracted to him not only because of his good looks but also because of his brilliant mind and endearing character. She was washed with uncontrolled waves of joy and simply took both his hands and brought them to her lips and kissed them with sparkling eyes. "I am happy for you, truly happy."

He was in total awe of her reaction, and while looking into her eyes, his own eyes filled with tears. "You can't imagine what it means to me to share it with you." It took him a minute to compose himself. Then their drinks and food arrived, and they both ate their fresh sandwiches with great relish.

"I have million things to attend to now that I am back home, but I shall be around more."

She simply said, "Oh, good," and he laughed. When they finished eating, they found out that the skies had cleared and the air was crisp and fresh. He put his arm around her waist and sucked in her warmth and alluring scent.

"You won't forget to tell me if you ever want to change your favorite perfume and try something else?"

She looked at him questionably, but he buried his face in the mass of her hair and mumbled, "Don't worry. I love your Dior. But I would love to buy you something else, and I don't know what." She giggled and turned around in his arms and gave him a long kiss on his lips. Though he was surprised, he seized the moment and pulled her closer to him and deepened the kiss. They just stood there on the sidewalk, oblivious to everything else.

However, it began raining again, and Michael knew they would get soaking wet if they didn't hurry to their cars. He detached himself from her by force, and holding her hand, they rushed to the parking lot. Sarah declined a lift home and said she had to get home and work on some article before she finished some papers for the next day. Though Michael was reluctant to leave her, he could see the logic of her words.

Just before he left her car, he said, "Why don't you call me when you have some spare time and we shall meet?" She looked at him quizzically, but then he smiled. "You don't even have my phone number or address, do you?"

She nodded her head, and he took out of his wallet a card and gave it to her. "Call me anytime you feel like talking to me … or for anything else, okay?" She smiled in consent, and he gave her a big kiss before he left the car and disappeared in the darkness.

Despite all her attraction to Michael, Sarah would not ring him, though her thoughts would wander to him quite often during the days. When it happened at work, his memory would spark a smile in her eyes, and she would linger for a moment on his kiss or his fingers in her hair; however, she would soon refocus and continue with her work. There was no point in fantasizing about him. He was a real person after all. In fact, she disliked daydreaming and going to unmapped regions of her heart and mind when it came to men. Sarah knew she wanted to see him very much and was interested in him as a mate, but she decided not to chase him. She believed she had conveyed her feeling for him in many ways—that she was interested in him and found him desirable.

The trouble came at night when she lay in bed and wondered where he was, what he was doing, and whether he would call her soon. Deep in her heart she knew that Michael would return. For one thing he had said so himself, and she believed him. For another it was obvious that he was attracted to her too. But still she listened to the wind and rain outside her home and remembered them kissing in the rain after the restaurant.

"Can I see you tonight?" It was Friday morning when he called, and Sarah was busy pottering around her home. As was her custom, she said yes but didn't ask where or when. "I have to be at my parents' home, and then I'll come. Is it okay with you?"

She always wondered why he asked her this question. "Yes, Michael, it is fine with me, and I'm looking forward to seeing you."

Chapter 18

The house was warm, and there was lovely, soft music in the background. Though it was still raining lightly, Sarah decided not to wait for Michael at her own house but to go and see her family at her father's house. She knew her brother and his family were there too. She left a short note for Michael on the door and darted to the next house.

It had been her parents' home since she was born, and her father had been living there with his second wife for a few years. Ruth was an impressive woman. She was tall, slim, and well groomed. She had short, salt-and-pepper hair that matched her gray eyes. She always looked as if she had just come out of a beauty salon, but in fact, she was a wonderful housewife and a partner to her father. She held a high position in the ranks of civil servants, and both David and Sarah loved her dearly because she made their father happy and was a decent person.

The house was warm and smelled of good cooking. Her brother, David, was stretched on the carpet with his baby daughter lying peacefully on his belly while her father was horsing around with the boy. She felt warm and welcomed and soon joined Ruth and Mira in the kitchen. She kissed her sister-in-law and gave Ruth a warm hug. They were about to eat dinner, which was good because Sarah was famished. She loved the sound of the babies and different smells of the food and felt utterly relaxed after the grueling week.

Her father was content in his marriage with Ruth, and he looked his good old self. He was tall and slim with some graying hair and the same loving smile in his brown eyes whenever he looked at his family. He was proud of his son and his work in the burgeoning electronic company and adored the two babies. Sarah was still the apple of his eyes, and he was aware she was going through a special phase but refrained from asking anything. He knew she would come forward and let them know when she was ready. Dinner was delicious, and they were taking their coffee when there was a knock on the door.

Michael was holding a beautiful bunch of dripping red roses, and his wet black hair was plastered to his head while his brilliant blue eyes were seeking her in the room. Sarah thought he looked so endearing and wonderful that she missed a heartbeat.

"I am Michael Goren, and I have come for Sarah." Her father was stunned, and so were the others. They knew nothing about a man in Sarah's life. It was Mira, David's wife, who had the presence of mind to approach Michael and take the roses and his soaking coat from him.

Sarah passed her sleeping nephew to his father and kissed Michael on his wet lips. She knew her actions would convey the right message to her family. She introduced him to everybody, and from that moment onward it seemed as if he had been part of the family forever. Her brother and Michael found common acquaintances, and her father seemed to know about Michael and his new invention and his father's electronic business. Sarah could see him looking at her surreptitiously from time to time, but she also discerned approval in his eyes.

This was the first time that Sarah had agreed to officially introduce any of her boyfriends to her family, and they all realized at once that she was serious about Michael. Ruth was a gracious hostess and offered him something to eat, but he declined, saying he had just come from a meal with his parents. However, he joined them with the coffee and cakes. Sarah knew she would have to speak with her father about Michael but left it all for another time.

After half an hour or so Sarah said they had better go, and they both took their leave under a huge umbrella. Ruth reminded them of the roses, but they both told her to keep them for herself. They rushed in the pouring rain and reached her home, squealing with laughter like two adolescents.

Inside the house it was warm and cozy, and they each quickly peeled their wet coats onto the floor. They were both panting from the rush in the rain, and Michael just held her head in his hands for a moment and then planted a big passionate kiss on her lips. Sarah was caught in his heat and ready to join his urgent need for her. She put her arms around his head and simply melted into him. Michael pulled the wet strands of hair from her face and kissed her eyes, her nose, and her eyebrows and then just buried his face in her neck while he lifted her from the floor. Sarah was a tall woman, yet Michael felt how light and supple she was as she stretched along his body. She giggled and stroked his hair.

"I have wanted to hold you like this for a long time. You are so beautiful, and I can't take my eyes off you." He looked at her adoringly, and his eyes were misted. He took off his glasses and put them on the side table.

"You are not so bad-looking yourself, Mr. Michael, and I have wanted to be with you too for quite a while." Sarah looked at him half seriously and half in jest. He slowly pulled her down along his torso, and she was delighted. "So I am Mr. Michael now, am I?"

"What do you want me to call you? darling or sugar pie?" Sarah became serious. "I want you to simply want me, and I will come. It would be enough." He bent his head and devoured her mouth. Sarah reciprocated with kissing his face and digging her fingers into his hair.

It was a turning point for both of them, and the atmosphere between them was changing. Sarah realized she had desperately missed him during the time she didn't see or talk to him. She missed his physical presence near her and especially his smiling, burning eyes behind his glasses when he looked at her. She knew Michael was special and he had more to him than just good looks and an inventive mind. He was becoming her mate, and she wanted him to be more.

They both clung to each other for a while, and then Michael's serious expression changed into something less somber. He said, "What do you fancy doing? Shall we go out to a pub, or would you first like to come to my house and see where I live?"

It was the first time Michael spoke about anything private from his life or suggested a visit to his home. Sarah was very curious to see his home and how he lived. Up to now they had only met at the university, her home, or some public places. "I would love to see your home," she said simply, and they both put on their rainwear again and grabbed the big umbrella by the door.

By the time Michael went to get the car, Sarah took a fresh loaf of bread she had baked in the morning and put it in her bag. Baking bread was one of her more favorite pastimes. It relaxed her, and the smell of yeast and warm bread filled the house with aromas that reminded her of her childhood with her mother at home.

In the cozy warmth of his car she offered him a piece of warm bread, and he simply relished it. She told him how much she liked to bake, and he said how he liked to eat fresh bread more than cakes or other foods.

Sarah was surprised to discover that he had been living in a house and not an apartment. It was a lovely villa tucked away in the middle of a huge and rather neglected garden, but it was in a quiet section of the town too. The whole road was lit with quaint lanterns hidden among tall leafy trees. Everything was glistening in rainwater, and there was a special, peaceful ambience to the neighborhood. There were no fences and no gates to the houses, and Michael parked in the front garden. He dashed to the front door, and only after lighting the garden and front porch did he ask her to get out of the car and enter his home, which was warm already.

Sarah didn't know what to expect. On the one hand, Michael was a modern young man, and from his clothes and behavior she surmised he would live in a modern environment; however, what she saw at first glance was a sedate European living room with beautiful heavy furniture and dark curtains. Michael could see her surprise and smiled.

"This is my grandparents' home, and as they both passed away and left it for me, my parents suggested I live here until I decide where I wish to settle down. By the way, my brother, Ben, also owns an apartment my grandparents left him, so we are both fine, you see." He took her hand and pointed out different photos of his grandparents, his parents, his brother, and himself.

"I love this house because I spent many happy years here with my mother's parents." He continued with a wistful smile, "There was a time when I was in high school when I spent few years with these two wonderful people. They were more than just grandparents to me. My parents had been away abroad for a few years with my younger brother, and I preferred to finish my studies here, so my grandparents took me into their home and looked after me like a pair of doting parents."

Sarah was fascinated by this whole new turn in her perception of Michael. She knew he was bright and successful and very popular, and she liked him more than she realized up to now; however, what she saw and heard from him now gave a new depth and dimension to his character and background. He had family and grandparents and memories that she was not a part of. Michael seemed to sense her confusion and led her to the kitchen, where to her surprise she found a state-of-the-art kitchen equipped with the most up-to-date kitchen equipment and utensils.

"My grandmother liked to cook and bake too, so although they had not renovated the house in recent years before they passed away, she insisted on having the best of all modern kitchens. In fact, just until a few months before she died, we used to dine here every Friday or Saturday. She always cooked some new gourmet dish to our delight. In fact, she once won the best cook competition for a women's magazine when I was very young." Michael was amused and confounded too to see her surprised face. "I promise you she was a very nice lady and you would have liked her."

In fact, Sarah was greatly surprised and in awe to hear Michael speak about his grandmother. Her own mother was an avid cook and baked beautiful pastries. She herself loved to try new dishes, but Michael never gave her even an inkling that he cared about food and domestic matters. She looked at him bemused and smiled. What's more, she didn't have any distinct memories of her grandparents. They had all died by the time she was young, so she missed the warmth, love, and a load of memories that grandparents can leave with you for life.

"You are a man of surprises. What else have you been hiding from me?"

"I can make a mean omelet, iron all my shirts, and my father says my steaks are the best."

'You are a man of all seasons, aren't you? An inventor, a mathematician, a chef, and good looking, and you dance very well too. Well, I have much to match, I am afraid."

Sarah looked at him teasingly; however, his face turned serious, and he took her into his arms and lifted her face with his hands. "You have just about everything a man wants, you know that?" His eyes misted behind his glasses, and he looked at her tenderly. "You are beautiful, talented, bright, and so poised that it kills me every time I tell you something exciting or surprising and you keep your calm and flow with whatever comes your way. And above all—" He paused for a second, and then removing strands of lustrous honey-streaked hair from her face, he whispered in her ear, "You are the sexiest woman I know and very desirable."

He hid his face in her hair, and she found herself leaning into his embrace and clinging to his firm body. It was the first time that Michael had ever expressed explicit interest in her physically. She knew he was drawn to her as she was attracted to him, but what he had said was not just mere words. There was a wealth of emotions and needs behind them, and Sarah felt great joy in her mind and body.

It was wonderful to feel desirable and sexy by this incredible man. She felt his arms tighten around her, and she lifted her face to him and kissed him on his lips.

"You are so sexy you can't imagine." After a moment of surprise Michael just lifted her long, supple body in the air and whirled her around the room.

"So you like me?"

"Of course I like you, you idiot." He just kissed her eyes and held her close to his body.

"Look, I know what I really want to do now, but we shall do it another time. I want us to go out and find a place for us to drink and dance. I want to celebrate." He looked beseechingly into her smiling eyes, and once he saw her approval, he turned to take their coats and umbrella and turn off all the lights. He went into the soft rain and walked toward his car.

They drove to his favorite club in silence, each absorbed in their thoughts, and after they ordered their drinks, they huddled in a corner table and listened to the music. Sarah was quiet and looked absorbed in the lyrics of the young singer and the soft music of the band, but she was basking in the warmth of Michael's words. Yes, he was her man. She looked at the strands of black hair falling on his face, his big bright eyes behind the glasses, his firm body, and his arm, which held her firmly, and she felt a wonderful tingle run along her spine. He was so exciting, so virile, and yet he was not aware of it.

She lifted her face and her luscious moist lips beckoned him to her. Looking at her, his body tensed with an electrical jolt, and he bent to kiss her and tried to satiate his hunger for her a bit. He kissed her lips and injected his tongue into the fountain of her mouth and sucked her breath away.

"Don't look at me that way again in public. I don't know if I can be responsible for my actions." She gasped for air, and he turned his face away from her.

"I think we can dance a little now that the music has changed. Would you like to?"

"Let me get my breath back, and please warn me next time beforehand if you are short of air and need mine." He chuckled quietly. "Come, let's dance. I need to feel you along my whole body now that I have stolen your breath."

As they were dancing a fast swing, they met some of Sarah's friends, and the whole evening turned into a big party. Introductions were made, and Michael was introduced to a bunch of young people who had been friends with Sarah since high school. They were very happy to meet them and joined in the revelry. After some time, however, a new bunch of guys joined the party, and among them was one new dancer. For a moment Sarah had a glimpse of sparkling blue eyes with an impish grin and a mass of unruly blond hair. It was Guy—young, happy, and vibrant. Sarah froze on the spot. He was dancing like Guy used to dance, and it was uncanny. The next moment she realized her mistake and felt how her heart missed a beat. Michael had just caught her in his arms and instinctively felt her distress. He led her unobtrusively from the dance floor and just let her gain her composure again.

"Are you okay? You look as if you have seen a ghost." He held her in his arms, and her face was pressed to his chest.

"Yes, I thought I saw a ghost, but I am fine now." She was still lost in her thoughts but seemed to have recovered her composure. Although Michael was curious to know the identity of her ghost, he refrained from pressing her. She was upset for some reason, and he knew she would tell him about it when she was ready. Sarah had just seen Guy's younger brother, who was five years older now and resembled Guy like a twin, but thank goodness he didn't recognize her.

Chapter 19

They finished their drinks and said good-bye to their friends. The air outside the club was fresh, and the skies were dark but cloudless with sparkling stars. It was lovely to walk along the riverbank and inhale the scent of the trees and grass after the rain. They walked toward their car and held each other tightly. Sarah stopped for a minute and gulped into her mouth the fresh air and then kissed him and blew the fresh air into his mouth. Michael stopped in his track and burst out laughing.

"Are you feeding me with fresh air?"

"Yes. I thought you don't get enough." She seemed to have gained her good spirits and was dancing around him.

"Isn't it just wonderful to breathe the fresh air after the rain?" He caught her hands and looked into her sparkling eyes.

"Yes, it is, and you are lovely too. But we'd better hurry, or the rain will catch us again."

In the car he put on some soft jazz music, and Sarah reclined her head on the seat with closed eyes. The soft music, the drinks, and Michael's arm on her shoulder made her feel good and relaxed. The memory of Guy was sweet and sad, but here was Michael with his charismatic mind, gorgeous body, and loving nature. She opened her eyes and said, "I am happy." He was amazed because he didn't expect anything like this from her. She had this fantastic ability to shake whatever mood weighed upon her and see a core of light at the end of any situation. They had often discussed politics in the university and in general, and although she was fiercely against discrimination of any form or unnecessary cruelty, she would eventually propose some balanced solution and keep her optimistic view of life.

"Am I part of your happiness?" he asked with half a smile and she turned to him with a big smile.

"You are the center of my happiness, don't you know?" Sarah knew that whenever she thought of the future and the kind of life she would like to have, she always saw Michael in the center of it. The more she got to know Michael and thought about him, the more she fell in love with him. Michael felt humbled, and his whole being was flooded with joy.

"I think I would like to sample some of this happiness and see if I am the core of it, but let us get home first." Sarah shut her eyes again and quietly giggled to herself.

As they walked into her house, Sarah did not turn on the lights. Nor did she turn off the music. The living room was warm and cozy, and the drawn curtains revealed that it was beginning to rain again. Sarah took off her coat and shoes and went into the kitchen, and Michael stood by the porch glass doors and looked into the sheets of rain falling onto the ground. Sarah came to stand by him with two glasses of red wine.

"Whenever I see sheets of rain falling, it reminds me of the sea. In my mind rain is like the sea only with gaps between the drops."

Michael turned to look at her. "What a lovely image. How did you think about it?"

"I have had this image in my mind since I was a child when my mother would take me walking on the beach while it rained.

She told me the sheets of rain would eventually become the sea but the gaps between the drops would disappear."

"You are an amazing woman, and I am very happy I know you." He took their wine glasses and left them on the table very gently and then turned her around in his arms and kissed her. It was a gentle kiss at first but it soon turned into a combustible fusion of two bodies. Michael took off his glasses and turned his full attention to different features of her face. He kissed her lips and covered her eyes, nose, and cheeks with passionate little strokes of his hot lips while his hands got entwined in the long strands of her hair. He smelled her scent and tasted the flesh of her lips and tongue. His hands moved to her shoulders and chest. He buried his face between her lifted breasts, and a long groan escaped his mouth.

"Do you know how long I have been craving to do just this?"

Sarah was occupied with touching his face and dropping small kisses on him. She lifted her head and innocently asked him, "What stopped you?" There was that impish smile in her eyes, and Michael knew she was teasing him.

"I thought if you didn't make love to me tonight, I would scream." She held her hands out to him. "Come, lover boy. Come into my parlor and make love with me."

She led him into her bedroom, which was spacy and in semidarkness. The bed was big, and the floor was covered with small Persian carpets. The curtains were drawn, and the soft music was playing here too.

Sarah sensed that although Michael was passionate about making love to her, he would wait for her cue, so she began taking off his cloths one by one. He stood patiently and followed her movements as she slowly unbuttoned his shirt and with a flourish threw it on the floor. The whole time she looked into his eyes while her tongue licked her lips and she made sucking sounds.

She danced around him and put her hands on his hips from behind and caressed his body while her breasts brushed against his back and stocked the fire in his body. Next she stood in front of him, and her fingers played with his lips. She covered his face with her hair, and her hands crawled gently to his bulging front and caressed it. She could feel his zipper straining against her hands, but she didn't offer any release.

That was the last straw for Michael. His hands went around her shoulders and held her firmly close to him. His fingers deftly lifted her sweater off her head and immediately released her from her bra. He gasped with surprise and pleasure. He held her a little away from him and looked at the beautiful globes of her breast. Sarah was slender and trim and her breasts were full and round as those of a young girl.

"You are just beautiful." His eyes devoured her shape, and his hands were slightly shaking when he released her belt and let her pants fall to the floor. She stood in front of him with her flimsy black panties and just smiled. She wriggled her hips, and they fell on the floor too and revealed the golden tuft of hair between her thighs. Sarah didn't linger anymore but just opened his zipper and let him stand naked too. "You are an awesome man, Michael Goren, and I fancy you like hell." He didn't know whether he should cry or laugh.

Michael was bewildered by her guileless and natural approach to sex. He was not used to young women being free and in touch with their own sexual needs and even expressing or sharing those feelings and thoughts with their partners. This was the first for Michael, and he realized how unique and special Sarah was.

He walked around her, quite comfortable in his nakedness, and assessed her lovely features. "Every part of you is beautiful and lovely but your whole—" he said and then paused for a moment. "You are an Amazon, and I am crazy about you. And I am going to make love to you now."

"Oh, yes?" She pushed him onto the bed and straddled him at once. She bent her head on to him, and her mass of chestnut hair covered his face. She caught his lips and began kissing him. Michael was instantly excited. He caught her buttocks and pushed his pelvis against hers while his tongue fenced inside her mouth and licked her teeth. Her breasts were grazing his face, and he took each one separately into his mouth. The feeling of bliss was total. He had Sarah naked in his arms, and he was sucking her nipples. It sounded so adolescent, and he giggled to himself; however, he felt as if he were just in the gates of heaven.

Sarah noticed how his big blue eyes became more luminous and slightly unfocused when he caressed her face and hair and slowly went down along her breasts and her abdomen and reached the point where her belly and thighs converged into a tuft of smooth, silky hair. Sarah's body tensed once he touched her center and began dropping small kisses around it. She saw the look of wonder in his eyes and instinctively opened her legs and lifted her pelvis to him. He sensed her inviting gesture and smiled at her. His fingers and lips were probing yet gentle. He moved the hair from her pulsing vortex, and his fingers opened the lips of her vagina. He kissed the pulsing flesh with relish. He could feel the nectar of her body and sucked it in. Sarah was quickly reaching her peak.

Her hands left his head and shoulders and wriggled around his manhood, which was pulsing and pushing against her body urgently. She sensed his need for release and reached his penis and held him gently in her hands. It was big and powerful and had a mind of its own. Yet when Sarah began moving her fingers along its shaft, she felt it mold into her palms yet keep its intense form.

Michael's fingers were busy and probed her inner core and touching hidden corners. His fingers found her clitoris and pinched its delicate lips lightly, causing Sarah to emit a long groan. She directed his shaft toward the craving mouth of her vagina. Michael gave a big thrust and penetrated her inviting core. The feeling was fierce and thrilling for both of them. Sarah felt as if she was being filled with a molten rock, and Michael was engulfed with liquid fire.

The culmination of their union came after Michael had driven Sarah's body into frenzy with massive thrusts into her. Her remarkable natural skill to being tuned to their needs helped them both. Sarah held herself as long as she could, and then feeling how the lava was flowing along his shaft, she simply exploded. It took just a second for Michael to respond to her spilling orgasm and join her with his own wrecking convulsions.

Sarah wrapped her arms around Michael and engulfed him with her body. He rested his head on her breast and felt his thudding heart calm down and join Sarah's languid form.

They lay there for quite some time, and Michael felt how months of stress, hard work, and deep yearning for Sarah washed away from his body and mind and left him sated and happy. It was a feeling of light that lingered in his mind, and he knew it came from Sarah. He realized that in addition to her natural gift of giving, she was well experienced in sexual art.

"I don't know who tutored you in making love. But he must have been a master, and he must have loved you very much." Sarah was jolted from her reveries about how wonderful and satisfying it was to make love to Michael, but his words evoked old memories in her mind. She remained quiet for a while and then said, "Yes, I was lucky to have known him, and he was really good in many ways." She turned to him and rained little kisses on his face. She then laid her head on his chest and told him about the time when Guy died.

"Do you remember the young man with the blond hair and blue eyes we met at the dance club earlier this evening? Well, he was Guy's younger brother, whom I haven't seen for years." She continued telling him about Guy, his sudden death, a family friend, and how he had helped her get over one of the most difficult times of her life. She briefly told him also about the fact that he had carried her from being a girl into womanhood. She never disclosed Ethan's name, and Michael never asked.

Sarah paused for a moment, lost in her thoughts and memories, and then said, "I shall always cherish his generosity and love for me." She raised her head, and the old impish smile was back in her eyes. "But you, Michael Goren, are the man I want to make love to again, if you so desire."

An electric current ran along Michael's spine, and his whole body was charged. "You are looking for trouble, Ms. Sarah Keter, and if you are not careful, I shall demand my pound of flesh many more times."

Chapter 20

The new intimacy between them established a new kind of relationship in their lives. Michael became a regular at Sarah's home by the sea, and he got to know her family better. There seemed to be some distance between Sarah's father and Michael at first. The older man seemed to examine the young man in his daughter's life and weighed his worth before he accepted him as a suitable suitor, but it didn't take long before he told Sarah herself his opinion of Michael. "I don't think I could have found a nicer and more worthy man for my precious girl than Michael." Sarah was thrilled to hear her father's opinion. She respected his point of view and sought his approval. Sarah knew that she was falling deeply in love with Michael, and her family's approval of her choice was very important to her.

They were both busy at university and work, and Michael had his inventions and business to look after, but they met at least once or twice in the middle of the week and were together during weekends.

It was a cold December day when Michael called her at her laboratory and told her that his brother, Ben, was in town and that his parents would like to meet her. "They want to meet the one woman in my life, and my brother is keen to see whether you are as beautiful as I claim." She sensed he was a little nervous, but she was happy to meet his parents at last.

Michael had been away for two weeks before the dinner with his parents, and Sarah missed him very much. It was good to speak to him whenever he could snatch some free time from his work with IBM and his other business meetings, but she missed his physical presence in her life and his unscheduled visits to her home most.

Sarah told her father and Ruth about the dinner invitation and asked what to take them. Ruth had suggested sending them a bouquet of flowers in advance. Later Sarah was happy to see how pleased his parents had been with the thoughtful gesture.

Michael called for her early in the evening as she was finishing dressing up. He looked handsome and urban, and Sarah realized that each time she saw him she missed a beat in her heart. He wore a beautifully tailored dark blue suit she had never seen him wear before with a light blue shirt. He wore a silken Italian tie that Sarah had bought him. It was fashionably striped in red, blue, and white and he carried a lovely bunch of carnations. They looked at each other, and the next moment they were in each other's arms and kissing.

"I missed you so much you can't imagine," she whispered in his ears

He held her away from him for a moment and said, "Oh, yes, I can. I love you, Sarah, and I need you like breathing." His eyes shone behind his glasses, and he looked at her with sincerity. Sarah was speechless.

It was the first time Michael had ever said to her anything about love. She knew she loved him every day more than the day before but refrained from saying anything about it. Once she heard him, it opened floods of joy and tears, and she looked at him with loving eyes and said, "I love you too, Michael Goren. I love you very much, and I missed you very much."

He embraced her to himself and kissed her hair and eyes. "Come, see what I brought you. It is not perfume, as you already have a Dior and a Chanel No. 5. This time I brought you something that will go with your outfit this evening." It was a beautifully wrapped flat box that contained the most exquisite silk scarf by Hermes in lovely autumn colors of green, brown, and orange. He tied it around her neck, and she was thrilled. It was a perfect match for her light green woolen blouse and ankle-length, dark brown skirt with high-heeled boots.

Chapter 21

Michael's parents lived in a very spacious and beautiful apartment facing the sea and overlooking the city, which was blazing with shimmering lights. It was a cold, bright night, and one could see some distant lights of boats on the horizon. The living room was paneled on one side with huge French windows that gave a clear view of the western part of the city and the marina. It was furnished in muted colors of blue and gray, and the lighting was invisible yet very effective.

Sarah realized that a lot of thought and good taste had been invested in the decor. At one corner there was a sitting area with long, beautifully upholstered sofas and some armchairs in dark blue, and in the middle there was a square Carrera marble coffee table. The dining table was set with light blue damask tablecloth, silver cutlery, white porcelain dishes, and crystal glasses.

A prominent black piano was tucked at one side of the room, and someone was playing a Chopin prelude. It must have been Michael's brother, Ben. He just waved to her and continued playing.

Michael's mother was medium-sized woman around fifty and very fair. She had beautiful blue eyes, and her hair was professionally cut short and set. She wore a lovely black shift dress with a string of pearls and a pair of red pumps. Sarah liked the artistic touch and smiled. His father was stocky and not as tall as Michael. He had a head full of graying hair and a moustache. Sarah was surprised to see it because it was so out of fashion, and yet it suited him. She warmed up toward both of them because they didn't seem to care about looking fashionable and being conventional. Michael introduced them as Rachel and Jack, and they both welcomed her with open arms.

Sarah could see Michael's mother's approval of her apparel. She had put up her shining strands of chestnut hair and caught them all at the back of her head with a beautiful antique clasp that she had inherited from her mother.

Her skin was fresh and glowing, and she looked very appealing with her open smile and engaging manners. Ben had just left his seat at the piano and came toward her. He looked at her slim figure appreciatively and gave her a friendly peck on her cheeks and a brotherly hug.

"Well, well, well, so you are the Sarah who has snatched my big brother and turned him into a pussycat? Do you know how many girls rue the day he set eyes on you?"

Sarah was surprised to hear what Ben was saying in jest, but Jack, his father, was quick to retort, "I think Michael is very lucky to have found Sarah." He turned to his wife and asked her, "Don't you agree with me, dear?"

Rachel Goren looked at her younger son with warning eyes, but she smiled at Sarah and gave her a motherly hug. "We are all delighted to meet you, Sarah, at last, and we trust Michael to have found the best young woman there is."

Michael seemed to release the air he had held in his lungs at last and took Sarah under his arm in a possessive manner. "Let's see you find anybody half as good and beautiful as Sarah," he said to his brother in earnest.

"I didn't say I don't like her. She is really gorgeous," said Ben. Then he whispered a "sorry" to Sarah and hung his head.

"So you'd better keep quiet. Don't say another word. Where are your manners?" His mother scolded him as if he were a child. Ben looked at Sarah sheepishly and smiled, and Sarah felt she could love him as a younger brother she never had.

It was a pleasant and delicious meal. Michael's father served a new red wine from a famous winery in the north, and Michael's promise that his mother was a gourmet cook was quite true.

The first course consisted of pate la meson with homemade marmalade on small toasted triangles. It was followed with a delicious consume soup and thin noodles, and the main dish was a feast to the eyes. There were breasts of chicken wrapped around dried prunes and apricots soaked in Brandi and grilled in the oven. A plate of freshly fried Vienna Schnitzels made of veal, a deep ball of basmati rice, a whole leg of lamb baked in the oven with small potatoes and sage. There was another dish with fresh salad, and Sarah wondered who was going to eat all the food.

The good wine and good food made it easy to talk and break the ice. Sarah told them about her mother's death, her father's new wife, and how much both she and her brother loved and appreciated Ruth. She told them a little about her studies and the fact she lived next to her father and swam in the sea almost every day.

Sarah could see they were all very close and loved each other, and Michael respected his parents and felt protective toward his younger brother. At one point during the meal Michael turned to Ben and gave him a warning look. "You are going to pay for that remark of yours to Sarah very soon, so be careful."

Ben cringed in his seat, but Sarah came to his rescue. "It is fine with me. In fact, I take it as a form of compliment. Isn't that what you meant, Ben?"

He looked at her gratefully but kept quiet.

Sarah felt very relaxed and at ease. Ben told them some intriguing anecdotes about his musical studies and performances in London, and Michael tried to explain to his mother what exactly he had invented that it merited so much money he was about to get. "Mum, we still have a lot of work and experiments to make before we come up with the final product, but I know it is going to make life much easier for people to communicate with each other in the future. It is not going to be overnight, but I know where it is going to take us."

Then Michael went to tell them about how he and Sarah had met and about Professor Sharpstein's awkward question to Sarah. "After what she had answered him, I knew I had to meet this young woman who stood up to the formidable professor and even humbled him." Michael then went on to tell them about the question and Sarah's answer, and they all laughed.

"I know Professor Sharpstein quite well. He is quite a chauvinist, although his wife is a lovely lady. We both sit on the same charity board."

This came from Rachel, and Michael added, "He knew Sarah's mother and wanted to marry her, but she preferred her Sarah's father to him."

The Many Shades of Light

"Good for her. No wonder he hassles Sarah." It was Rachel again.

Sarah just nodded with her head and said, "Oh, he is harmless. And anyway, I love my dad. He is a great guy."

The rest of the evening passed pleasantly, and when they took their coffee, Ben went to the piano and began playing some popular tunes from musicals. Sarah went to stand beside him and joined him with the lyrics. She had a melodious voice, and they seemed to be in tune with each other. It had been a long time since Sarah sang in company, and Michael was pleasantly surprised to hear her sing. It was Michael's father, Jack, who joined them with his soft baritone, and then they all sang together.

When it was time to part, Sarah felt as if she had found a new family, and she departed from Michael's parents with the promise to see them more.

"Don't be a stranger. We would love to see you any time."

Then Rachel turned to her son and said, "Please give Sarah our phone number and urge her to come for visits even when you are not here." Michael was touched by his parents' gracious gestures toward Sarah. He kissed his parents good night and gave a hug to his brother.

They drove to Sarah's home, and Michael said he would love to drive along the seashore the next morning. He wanted some fresh air and total relaxation after the grueling days in the States. "I would also like to tell you about my invention and what I do in the States and here."

They spent the night in making passionate love and telling each other small tidbits about their pasts. Sarah told him about how impressed she was with his family and how much she liked them all.

"You like even Ben, I suppose?" he asked.

"Why even Ben? I think he was embarrassed at first and said the first thing that came into his head. I didn't see anything wrong in his remark. Anyway, it disclosed a few things about you, my lover boy." Sarah smiled at Michael and caressed his face. "I didn't know you were so popular."

"I am not as half popular as you are, but it is over for both of us, isn't it?"

He looked at her somberly, and she just held his hand close to her heart and whispered, "I love you, Michael, and it is final with me. There are no ifs, ands, buts, or halfway with my feelings for you. I don't need another man in my life, and you'd better believe me."

Chapter 22

It was December, and the weather had turned very cold. They were both busy in their separate studies and work and didn't have much time to meet during the week but for short breaks to eat something before they went on with their respective lives. However, on Friday or Saturday nights he would always come with a bunch of lovely fresh flowers, and they would go out to eat or meet with friends.

Michael knew it was Sarah's twenty-fifth birthday on December 15, so he told her he would like to celebrate it with her. Sarah was too busy to consider the date very much, so she just had her hair done and bought a new pair of beautiful black leather boots to go with her brown designer suit. She added Michael's Hermes scarf to her ensemble. She told Michael she would meet him at her father's home, as they had asked them to pop in for a drink.

The house was unusually quiet and dark when she got there. She thought maybe she had made a mistake with the date but dismissed it. She heard a strange noise behind her but still opened the door. At once all the lights in the house went on, and Sarah was amazed to see her family and Michael's parents together with her brother's family all standing there, festively dressed and shouting, "Happy birthday!" As she walked in, Michael walked in behind her and said, "I was afraid you won't go in." Sarah was totally dazed from the lights, the flowers, the music, and the beautiful table set for dinner with many candles and balloons. She wasn't aware that Michael's parents had met her family, and she looked at them in amazement. Many kisses, hugs, and greetings were showered upon her, and she simply melted with it all. She realized Michael had worked hand in hand with her family and arranged the whole thing.

After a few minutes Sarah's father opened a chilled bottle of champagne, and they all toasted Sarah and wished her long life and happiness.

It was a tradition in her family to hand out the birthday presents at the beginning. First came her nephew and niece and offered her a poster they had prepared with pictures of the whole family, including Michael. She was touched. David and Mira gave her a lovely silver bracelet that she had liked. Michael's parents gave her a pair of small diamond earrings, and Ruth and her father gave her keys to a new mini minor. She was simply speechless. She had wanted to change her old mini to a newer model for a long time, but she didn't have the resources or the time to deal with it. It was just wonderful. She sat on her chair and simply sent an "I love you" toward them all.

It was time for Michael. He had nothing in his hands, and he just approached her with a very serious look in his eyes. Suddenly he bent down on his knees, and to the amazement of all present, he extracted a small box from his pocket, opened it, and showed it to Sarah. There was hush in the room, and they all looked at the sparkling pink diamond ring in it. Michael caught both her hands and said, "Sarah Keter, I love you with all my heart. Would you please do me the honor and be my wife?"

Sarah just looked at him in amazement and saw his love for her and realized it was the most important moment in her life. She was oblivious of all the others and had eyes only for Michael. She forwarded her the finger of her left hand to him and said, "Michael Goren, I love you with all my heart, and I would be honored to be your wife." She could hear Michael breathe in, and all the rest began clapping their hands. He put the ring on her finger and simply took her in his arms and kissed her.

They finished few bottles of champagne that night, and Sarah thanked each one separately for the gifts they had given her. She was also surprised to find out that no one knew about Michael's intention to propose to her.

Chapter 23

They decided to get married after Sarah had completed her postgraduate studies and after Michael had finished his PhD papers in the summer, and then they wanted to move to Michael's house, as it would be more convenient for all concerned.

A week before the wedding night Michael went away to the States, and just before he left, he presented Sarah with a sealed envelope and asked her to read it at home. She was slightly intrigued but only opened it at night before she went to bed. It was an official document from his lawyers that informed her that Michael had made her full partner in his promising electronics company and that he had also made her the only heir to all his wordily assets. Sarah was in total shock. The totality of the generous act bewildered her, and she decided to sleep on it before she talked to Michael about it.

Michael made it clear to her that it was final with him, and both his parents knew about it and approved of it. "You are going to be my only wife, so everything I have is yours too, but I would rather make it official." Sarah was humbled by his gesture and simply prayed for his safety.

The wedding was a joyful event and a lovely occasion to meet family and friends. After a short ceremony there was a ball and everybody danced with the bride and groom. Ben had arrived from London with his small band, and they had composed a beautiful new melody for the moments when Sarah and Michael made their vows to each other and then played a string of popular songs to the delight of all present.

As Michael was due to return to the States, Sarah decided to remain at home and postpone their honeymoon for another date.

It was a new sensation to be Mrs. Goren and be treated as a wife and a married woman. Sarah continued with her regular daily tasks of working in the lab at the university, carrying on with her research into her thesis, and beginning to mind the garden and the new house she began living in. Although it kept her busy, she missed Michael's daily presence very much. He did call her every day from wherever he was, but she missed hearing him whistle when he took a shower only at nights or bring her a cup of coffee to bed before she even opened her eyes. He told her he hated to shave, and unless he had a special meeting, he would walk around unshaved for a few days until Sarah or his mother told him off. He also once told her he liked it better when she let her hair down or walked around like a young colt with a reddish ponytail. So she hardly ever put her hair up, and he would smile at her with appreciation and gratitude. Sarah also began visiting Michael's parents when he was away, and she learned to appreciate them and realized once again how much she missed her own mother.

Sarah and Rachel were sitting in the garden and drinking some coffee and talking about Sarah's plans to revitalize the garden and begin the renovations of the old house.

"You know, Rachel, I fell in love with this beautiful house from the first moment Michael showed it to me, and I hope the changes we intend to make won't diminish its beauty and uniqueness." She paused for a minute and continued, "I hope you and Jack don't mind the changes we wish to make. In fact, both Michael and I intend to be very careful to preserve the old ambiance of the whole house and the neighborhood, but we have to update the old water installations and the electrical wiring if we wish to live here."

"Of course we don't mind." Rachel caught both Sarah's hands and smiled at her. "I think you would do a wonderful job with the renovations you plan, and we would both love to help you as much as you allow us. After all, Michael got it from his grandparents, and now it is your home."

Sarah beamed at her kind and supportive mother-in-law. "You can't imagine what it means to me to get your blessings for accepting me so graciously into your family." It was obvious that Sarah was emotionally moved by the older woman's support and affection toward her.

"My dear Sarah, it is us who are blessed to have you and your family as part of us. I have never seen Michael so happy and content in his life. You know, although he has always been very successful in his studies and inventions, I could always detect that something was missing there in his life, and since he met you, he seems to have become more in peace with himself."

Sarah's eyes were sparkling when she got up to kiss her gentle mother-in-law on her cheek. It was obvious that Rachel was quite moved too by the sudden show of love and continued, "I know that you and Michael have not really had a proper honeymoon, and you both deserve a much-needed holiday before you begin with the house and garden, so it crossed my mind—why don't you and Michael go on a delayed honeymoon somewhere in the United States and start with the house after you return?"

It was a brilliant idea, and Sarah was thrilled with the prospect of meeting Michael in New York.

After she discussed it with Michael on the phone, Sarah made all the arrangements through his office and flew by herself to New York and met Michael in his hotel. After a short delay they drove to the Niagara Falls and spent a week around the magnificent falls on both sides of the border and the countryside. It was a new experience for both of them. They had never spent more than a day or two together alone and always were busy with work, studies, or other people. Here they were in different motel rooms each night and free to do whatever they wanted. They were thrilled to go places and do things they both loved like eating ice cream in the middle of the night or cycling in the rain and not care about deadlines and tutorials.

Michael told her about his work and what he intended to do after he got his present invention on the market. They spoke about children, and Sarah said she would have liked to have a big family. They settled on three to five and began discussing names and genders. They were driving along a country lane in a peaceful area of the Hamish Land when Michael said, "You know, Sarah, as much as I want to have sons to continue my work and to play ball with as I used to do with my brother, Ben, I would love to have a couple of daughters. I never had a sister in my life and would love to be pampered by my beautiful wife and doting daughters." He had this devilish twinkle in his eyes, but Sarah's retort was not far to come.

"I agree. You need more love and tender care than you already get from everybody." She paused and fondly stroked his hair but then continued, "Why do you think that if you had only daughters, they would not be able to continue your heritage and succeed in running a highly sophisticated computer firm?"

Michael was stunned. He knew he had made a critical mistake when he singled out the boys as potential heirs to his work. He continued driving for few more minutes without responding to Sarah's loaded question. Then he stopped the car on a side lane and took both her hands in his and said, "My dear, first you are very right in your complaint, and I wish to apologize for what I had said to you and to my future daughters. I suppose I got carried away with all the regular clichés about boys in blue and girls in pink, but I want to solemnly promise you that I shall never discriminate between our children with regard to gender or on any other grounds. I promise to love and cherish them equally as much as I do their mother."

He looked at her sincerely with a deep concern in his eyes. "I know I have offended not only our future girls but also you and my mother, whom I greatly love and respect. Would you forgive me?"

It took Sarah a while to digest the whole impact of the discourse between them. She knew him well enough to be sure that he really regretted his sexist comment and that he would never let her down in that matter, but it had to be completely clarified between them.

"You know how much I care about these issues of gender and equality, so I am sure not to tolerate any signs of it within our family, but I do forgive you for what you said because I believe you are being honest and honorable."

She looked at him with a half-angry and half-tender look and then whispered, "I love you, and I trust you."

Michael's heart was suddenly filled with overwhelming joy with his young wife's generosity and trust. He bent over and embraced her as tightly as he could in the confined of the car. They kissed for a long time, and Sarah knew she had the right man beside her.

They were in a small hotel on the brink of the great falls, and it was impossible to talk or listen to music if the windows were not shut. They had spent a long drive to one of the Hamish picturesque villages and discussed their unique way of life. Michael said he couldn't live in such an environment, as he would not be able to suppress his inventive mind and curiosity and need for advanced technology.

"I think they live on another planet ... in a different century." He paused a little and continued, "Their lifestyle and values have great merit, but I couldn't live in such a limited environment."

Sarah agreed with him that the Hamish way of life would not suit everyone, but she thought it could be a good place to raise children. "Think about pollution. Think about the effect of television and think about the fact that technology creates some kind of social alienation in society and even among families."

"Well, it is our responsibility as parents to protect our children and teach them enough values so that they would follow the right way. Anyway, we will always be there for them, won't we?"

"Yes, my love, we shall always be there for them and for each other." She kissed him. "And where in a Hamish world would I find a resourceful and handsome lover like you?" she told him and rolled over him. She caught his head and showered him with kisses. She knew Michael would continue from there.

It was amazing how well tuned their separate bodies were when they just touched each other.

Sarah knew they were both tired after the long day, but Michael just turned her on her back with a flip of his arm and feasted his eyes on her naked body. He then diligently touched kissed and caressed each limb and part and when she was too frenzied to call his name, he penetrated her and joined their final dance. He knew exactly where her breaking point was and how he could make her reach her climax with him.

It was on their flight home that Michael first mentioned the incident with Professor Sharpstein during their wedding. Professor Sharpstein was of course invited by her father, and Sarah first saw him from afar. But at one stage of the ball she was being photographed with her whole family, and he suddenly joined the picture. On the surface he looked very chic and urban and kissed the bride and wished her good luck, but Sarah was aware of his ruddy face and watery eyes. What bothered her was his general posture and demeanor. She realized he was slightly drunk and didn't want to stand next to him. Suddenly the professor turned to Sarah and said, "So I was right when I said all you girls come to the university to catch yourselves husbands." There was total silence among the small crowd around them, and he went on, "I see you got yourself a winner this time." Then he turned to Sarah's father. Slurring his words with the effect of the whiskey he had been drinking all evening, he said, "You are a lucky dog, aren't you? You know she was supposed to be mine if you had not snatched her mother from under my hands." There was an embarrassing silence among the crowd near Sarah, and some guests were trying to pull the professor away.

Michael came to stand beside Sarah and her father, but it was Rachel, Michael's mother, who looked at him with contempt and said, "If she were your daughter, she couldn't possibly have been anything like our Sarah." It was the professor's wife who put her hand on his shoulder and took him out of the hall at last.

Although she was repulsed by the whole incident, Sarah felt sorry for the professor, as she knew he didn't have any children, but Michael was more indignant and angry.

"I am sorry we invited Professor Sharptein to our wedding. I know he is an old family friend, and I respect him very much as a professor. But he was rude and drunk during our wedding, and I don't think I would like to meet him in our home." Sarah could see that Michael was really furious about the whole incident and was amazed he had never brought it up between them before.

"I never said anything about it to you because it was your father who invited him and I greatly respect his wishes, but I believe his behavior was not entirely because of his gross consumption of alcohol but because of something much deeper."

"I must admit we were all embarrassed about the incident, but I feel sorry for him and his wife." She paused and held Michael's hands. "You see, although he is famous and successful in academic circles, I hear from my father they are both very unhappy because they don't have any children."

Sarah looked into Michael's stormy eyes, which gradually turned soft and calm, and said, "I shall try to keep away from him as much as possible in the future, okay?"

Michael bent his head and kissed his young wife on her lips. "You are wise. Let's forget about him."

Chapter 24

Returning to a new home and a new status was refreshing in itself after their very intensive honeymoon holiday. Michael went straight to his labs and his university duties, and Sarah began moving her personal belonging to Michael's home. Her father was very helpful, and Michael's parents lent her a hand anytime she needed one.

They decided to move her old piano to their new home too, as Sarah said she would have liked to practice again. It was a lovely house, and Sarah enjoyed most of all the modern conveniences of the kitchen. Her only regret was the state of the garden, and she decided to start cultivating it after the first rain. But first she had to clean it and prepare for new plants. She decided to take a break from continuing with her PhD and just accept the position of a junior lecturer in the math department of the university in the fall.

Sarah became aware of her pregnancy in early October and prepared a lovely supper for Michael before she informed him of the good news. He was thrilled. He simply carried her in his arms around the house and kept saying, "I am going to be a father. I am going to be a dad."

At the end of the fourth month they discovered they had twins, and they were in heaven. Rachel, Michael's mother, told Sarah that it was quite common in her family to have twins, so she was not surprised but extremely happy. The preparation of the house for the arrival of the twins was in full swing when Michael decided not to make an exit and sell his major shares in his company for a huge sum of money but rather to expand his firm and keep IBM as a minor partner.

Sarah's father told her it was a wise move, as the component Michael had invented would be used in many other electronic instruments. The shares of this company would be worth millions in few years. Now that they were going to have children, Michael said, they had better think about their future. "I want to leave them with enough so that they will have the time and means to come up with new innovations."

Sarah was surprised. "We are going to be here for them for many years, so don't worry about leaving them a legacy of money."

"It is more than money. It is a direction and an opportunity," Michael said seriously. Sarah wondered what had really prompted his decision but decided not to question him about it. She knew Michael would talk to her in due time.

Tom and Dona were born on a Friday evening, and Michael was in ecstasy. Although it wasn't the fashion at the time, he stayed with her in the delivery room the whole time and saw how his son and daughter were delivered into the world. Michael was not a religious person, yet he was in total awe when he looked at the faces of his newborn children and at his wife. Sarah was exhausted from the double delivery, and her eyes were bloodshot from sleepless hours of labor; however, she was smiling at him as if she had just given him a gift. He knew he was a blessed man and prayed a little prayer for their safety.

Tom and Dona were wonderful children—bright, active, and full of life. Though they were different in their looks, they had a lot in common. Tom was fair with lovely gray eyes, and Dona had a head full of chestnut hair like her mother with the piercing blue eyes of her father. It was clear from the start that the children shared some uncanny bond between them, a bond that enabled them to read each other's minds from an early age. Whenever one of them began to cry, the other would nudge the twin and make him or her stop, and Sarah often found their fingers twined.

As they grew up, they constantly talked and whispered things to each other, and even their parents couldn't tell what they were saying or plotting. Quite often they were full of mischief and played pranks on their family and friends. Michael and the two sets of grandparents simply adored them.

Michael suggested they expand the house in the back and add two more bedrooms and an open porch around the house. It was left to Sarah to oversee the work and keep the children away from the workers.

Chapter 25

Older Sarah

Now that I look back on the time after my marriage and the birth of the twins, I consider it among the best periods of my life. I had begun the third phase of my studies. I had a good job at the university, and Michael and the twins just filled my cup of happiness to the brim. I was thrilled with the miracle of birth and the growing of my two bright babies. They were a daily source of joy and wonder for both Michael and me. Each day brought new discoveries for all of us, and I was content to go on with my life.

Yet when I consider my work and children, I realize it was Michael's presence in the center of my life that gave me the most joy and meaning. I have seen enough broken marriages and partnerships to cherish what I had, and I often wondered what the secret of our success was.

Reflecting, I think it was mainly due to the fact that Michael and I were compatible in many ways—our background and education, our good looks, and our inner strength. But most of all it was due to our mutual respect for each other and our trust in each other. I thought Michael was much more than an attractive, successful male who provided for my children and me. He was a full partner in my life. I loved Michael because he was a decent human being who treated me with mutual love and respect.

I remember we had a lot of disagreements about members of our families or friends, about other people's codes of behavior, and about politics. But we were in full agreement about how we should raise our children and their education and about how to spend money.

Money and education were two issues on which we always agreed before we made any major decision. As we both worked and contributed to the welfare of our family in our respective jobs, we always listened carefully to each other in these matters.

And yes, we were quite compatible in regard to sex too. In all the years Michael and I were together, we didn't cease to be attracted to each other. Even when I was pregnant, we would indulge in sex games, and Michael always told me I was sexier than ever.

As a grown-up woman, I still cherish my body as I was taught to do by my parents when I was young. I also never let anybody abuse my right on my body. I believe I was lucky to be initiated into the realm of sex by a master like Ethan, but my whole approach to sex considers it as a wonderful and exciting activity that should be practiced freely and with full consent of anyone involved. Sex can bring a lot of pleasure and is necessary to life, but it can also be destructive and pitiable as we often witness around us.

The other day I had mentioned the presence of my ethereal visitor, Ariel, to a lady in my circle of friends. First she looked at me in disbelief that I could still engage in deriving pleasure from sexual activities and then accused me of being depraved. As I listened to her, I realized she couldn't have possibly been able to give full pleasure to any active partner in her life, and neither had she ever fully enjoyed any sexual intercourse. I went on to talk about the weather with her.

The other matter that has occupied my mind all those years was the absence of my mother in my life. I remembered how wonderful and attentive she was to my brother and me and how she knew what was essential and what was trivial in our education. Although I did share almost every moment of my own children's childhood with Michael, I also craved for my mum to share the fruits of her own work in my children. Rachel was a wonderful and considerate mother-in-law, and I was more than lucky to have her beside me. So were Ruth and Mira, David's wife, and I am grateful to all of them. However, I did miss my own mother and still do. I suppose it stems from our ingrained need to always get our mum's approval and be under her umbrella no matter what we do or what age we are.

Chapter 26

Young Sarah

In October Sarah began the academic year with a class of new math students. Most of them were male, and Sarah was unhappy about it. She also noticed that most of the students were skeptical about her credentials and her ability to teach such a prestigious course, but after few attempts to tackle her with tricky questions, they settled down to some serious studies. She wasn't angry with any of her male students for trying to make a fool of her, but it was sad that they couldn't accept the probability that a woman could be good in math and academically qualified to teach them. Though they were still young, they already suffered from serious gender prejudice.

It was December, and she was still nursing both babies. The morning was clear and very cold, and she had a tutorial at nine and was going to be late. After she gave last instructions to the nanny, she washed and put on her light brown silk blouse. She wore her ankle-length woolen skirt and black boots too. She combed her long strands of hair into a ponytail and put a green barrette on top. She took her coffee-colored leather jacket and went to her car.

When she walked into her class, some students whistled and made catcalls. Sarah resented their reaction (which part of her expected) but decided to ignore it. She just smiled and asked them to channel their excitement into solving the math problem she had given them the lesson before. She was aware of the disquiet in the class.

Just before the weekend Sarah had given her students an equation to solve and dared them to do it on their own. She knew it wasn't fair to give them that question, as it was hard and they had not learned the material that could help them solve it, but Sarah wanted them to realize that though they considered themselves the toast of the town, they had still a lot to learn. She turned to the board and wrote the long equation on it while she explained each stage.

They all began to grumble and talk, but suddenly one of the students called her name. It was Alex, the new guy from overseas. He hardly ever said much but always got straight A's on his tests. Sarah had noticed him from the beginning. He was not very tall, but he was stocky in built. He had very soft and curly auburn hair, which reached his collar, and most of the time he wasn't shaved. His eyes were black, and he always stared at her even when they met in the corridors or cafeteria.

"Yes, Alex, what seems to be the problem?"

"I think it is possible to solve this equation in a different way." He just sat there and looked at her while the rest kept quiet.

"Would you care to show us all on the board how you do it?" She could see he was reluctant to get up and come to the board, but then other students dared him to do it, so he got up and made his way to the front of the class. Sarah realized he was embarrassed and ill at ease, so she handed him the chalk. He looked at her for a moment, and then his glance dropped down to her chest. He had a strange look in his eyes, and Sarah felt a sudden chill.

She knew she looked beautiful and well groomed and her figure had returned to its former shape, so she looked into his eyes expectantly and wondered what had attracted his attention so deeply. She could see the blush creeping up his face, and he looked quite miserable. He was standing there with his back to the board, and she stood facing him.

It was the blessed bell that saved both of them. Once he heard the first sound, he put the chalk on her desk and rushed out of the room. Sarah was bewildered with his reaction and lost in thought. She dismissed the class, took her jacket, bag, and papers, and hurried out after him, but he was nowhere to be seen.

She remembered Michael had promised to meet her in his office for lunch, and she was glad to be in his comforting company.

Before entering his office she went to refresh her makeup and looked at herself in the mirror. Her hair looked fine under the green barrette, and her face was flushed a little. But her cheeks were rosy, and her skin shone. She was quite presentable. Then she took off her jacket, and a cry escaped her lips. There were two wet spots on her beautiful silk blouse exactly where her nipples were. She was shocked and mortified. In the rush of the morning she had not used the special pads to cover her nipples after she had breastfed the babies. She wondered how long she had the stains and who else among the students had noticed them. Now she understood Alex's stare and embarrassment. How was she going to walk into her class again, let alone meet Alex?

When she told Michael, he didn't laugh. He was well aware of Sarah's need to maintain her high standard of appearance and looks. He kissed her and pulled her into his arms. "I realize it is embarrassing for both of you, but Alex seems to be a grown-up guy and must know you have babies. So just apologize to him and continue with your teaching as if nothing has happened."

She looked up into his face and said, "I am mortified and ashamed. I pray the rest of them didn't notice it."

The next lesson Sarah asked Alex to hand out his solution to the problem in writing, and that was that. She didn't get any reaction from Alex, and he didn't mention it. It seemed that none of the other students was aware of it. Sarah breathed a sigh of relief. She realized it was a narrow escape and was determined never to repeat it.

Chapter 27

Tom and Dona were celebrating their fifth birthday, and the whole family was gathered on the beautiful lawn in the garden and on the porch. It was a festive occasion, and the premises were decorated with balloons and special lighting. There was a friendly football game going between grown-ups and children, and the winners got all the trophies and extra ice cream. It was after they had all settled down to relax and enjoy the cool evening that Michael and Sarah decided to inform their extended family of Sarah's pregnancy.

They called Tom and Dona to stand beside them, and Michael said, "We are happy to inform you that we are expecting an expansion to our family. However, this time we have more good news." Michael paused a moment and continued with a serious face, "However, this time Sarah is pregnant with twins again." There was a moment of total silence, and then there was clapping and whistling and cheerful whistles.

"At this rate you can have a basketball team in two and a half pregnancies. Well done, sister," David said, and the whole crowd began laughing.

The next twins were born on a Friday evening on another day in the middle of November, and they were all thrilled.

That next night after Tom and Dona were left with their grandparents, Sarah fed her new twins, washed herself, and lay in her bed in a fresh new gown. She closed her eyes in the dim light of her room and relaxed. The private room was filled with many different flowers, all of which had been arriving since morning. Suddenly she could feel Michael sitting next to her, and she could see he was excited in his quiet way. Once again there was a knock on the door, and a new delivery arrived with the most incredible bouquet of red roses. The flowers included a letter and a small delicately wrapped box.

Sarah looked at the long-stemmed red roses and smiled at Michael. She just wondered who had sent her such an elaborate gift. She opened the small box, and inside was a magnificent diamond bracelet with matching earrings. Sarah knew something about diamonds, as Michael had showered her with expensive gifts on every occasion, but these were just fabulous. She looked at him and then opened the envelope. The note read,

> My darling Sarah,
>
> Thank you for bringing so many shades of light into my life.
> I love you with all my heart.
>
> Your loving husband,
> Michael

Sarah just sat there in silence and stared at Michael, who couldn't decipher her reaction, and then she simply burst out crying. She was bewildered and overwhelmed with his generosity, his boundless love, and his total support. He was the love of her life, the beacon that led her safely every day, and he was thanking her!

"Oh, Michael, I love you so much, and I just can't see life without you."

His body sagged, and he bent toward her and kissed her lips, her eyes, and her hair. Then he cried with her a little. At last he said, "Aren't we a little mad? We have two new beautiful babies, and we just sit here and cry."

She caressed his face with her hands and then laid her head on the pillow and closed her eyes. "What shall we call them?" she asked.

"I suggest we ask the children to choose," Michael replied, and that is how it was done. Dona wanted to call the firstborn Laura, and Tom settled for Arik.

Chapter 28

Dora was about sixteen when she came to live in the Goren's' house and help Sarah with Tom and Dona. She was brought up in many foster homes, and Sarah found her one night helping another older woman to clean her lab at the university while training to be a domestic help worker. Dora was a neat young woman who hardly remembered her mother and had no idea who her father was too. Dora had been left sitting on the doorstep of a foster home somewhere in a village in the north, without any identifying details apart from her name and age. She was five years old at the time and called Dora.

Sarah was pregnant at the time with Tom and Dona and felt strong feelings for the young girl who didn't dare lift her eyes to look at her. She was afraid Sarah would report her to the authorities. Dora was of medium height with very light auburn hair pulled back from her face with pins. She had deep brown eyes and a lovely smile. After she helped her with the welfare offices, Sarah suggested Dora come and help her with the house chores. Dora was deeply happy and grateful to come and work for the Goren family. Once the twins arrived, she helped Sarah in everything and finally came to live with them. She had a weekly day off and could further pursue her studies. It was a satisfactory arrangement for all, and now that Laura and Arik had come, she had a handful.

Michael had built her a special separate unit on the corner of the garden, and it was Dora's domain. When she first went to live there, she simply cried. She said it was the first time in her life she had had a place of her own. The kids adored her, and both Sarah and Michael trusted her implicitly. They treated her as a full member of the family, and she always ate with them at the table. The only thing she insisted on was never getting married.

Though Michael was considered an innovator and a rich man, it didn't change much in their daily life. They still lived in the same house with the sprawling garden and continued being a close-knit family. Though Michael was busier than ever before, he always found time to be with his wife and children despite his travels and workload. They celebrated holidays and birthdays with grandparents and friends and often went on holidays together. Sarah had finished her dissertation and completed her PhD around December, but she decided not to continue her work at the university.

At one stage Michael told her he would have liked her to join him in the expanding firm he had established and get involved with the work. "I need your rationale and unique input in what I am planning to do. I need you to be beside me and get to know all the ropes because I trust you." He told her all this one day out of the blue and, and though Sarah was surprised, she liked the idea and became an integral part of the firm.

It had been Michael's dream since childhood to travel to South America and visit the area of Patagonia and Argentine after he had read the adventure book *The Children of Captain Grant* by Jules Vern. He often told Sarah how wonderful it would be if they could travel there and then go up to the Iguassu Falls between Argentine and Brazil.

The children were twelve and seven, and they were doing very well at school; however, Sarah noticed that Michael was showing signs of strain in his face, and he wasn't sleeping well. She found out from his schedule that he was about to travel to the States in a month, so she organized it with everybody concerned that Michael would be away for two more weeks for a holiday. She planned to meet him in New York, and they would travel from there to their destination.

Michael was in shock when he saw Sarah in his hotel room in New York at the end of his stay there. He was sure he was flying back home, but Sarah put him right. At first he wasn't sure he could make it with all the workload and appointments that were scheduled for him, but once he understood that all had been taken care of and he was as free as a bird, he gave one long sigh of relief and simply fell on the bed and carried Sarah with him.

"You are so fantastic and so wonderful. How did you know I needed just this?"

He looked at her in wonder, and she simply lay beside him and said, "I know you, my love, and I see how tired you are lately. We both need some quality time and not to worry about the children or work."

He stroked her hair and face and whispered in her ear, "My wise wife, my beautiful, wise wife," and fell asleep.

The whole trip was magical because Sarah had thought about every step and every minute of their time. Michael was thrilled with her choice and showed great knowledge of the area and its history. He said that for him it was like a dream come true to follow Captain Grant and his children's adventures and see this remote area of the world.

He filled her ear with massive data about the difficult and harsh terrain of the area, about the early conflict between Argentine and Chile and how they resolved it, about Magellan, who discovered the tip of South America in 1520 and expected the natives to be giants.

Sarah remembered when her father had returned from his trip to Brazil during the summer when Guy died. He was very upset and sorry for her grief, but not long after that, he told David and her some fascinating details about his adventures around the Iguassu Falls and the jungles of Brazil. He had taken masses of pictures and showed them his local guides and huge anaconda snakes on the trees along the Amazon River. She remembered him say, "You know, Sarah, I have been fantasizing about going to the places where Captain Grant traveled and where he met his children my whole life. Your mother and I had planned to do it some time, but as you know, it was impossible." Her father sounded enthusiastic and happy and looked young and wistful at the same time.

"Unfortunately I did not have time enough to fly to Chile and Patagonia this time. Well, maybe some other time." Sarah remembered his smile and told Michael about it.

"I am so happy you planned this trip for now," Michael said. "You see, it is the best time of the year, and it will not be as cold as Captain Grant and his crew had to suffer." He took a short breath and continued, "From the itinerary you have showed me, I see we are going to be in Patagonia, which is a Spanish word meaning 'big foot,' and Magellan used it to describe the native people in the area. I am so excited to get there." He turned to Sarah and gave her a big hug and a kiss. "You know, one day we will take the kids with us on such a trip. What do you say?"

Sarah burst into peals of laughter. "We are on the first leg of our tour, and you are already planning another one?"

"My dear, let me dream ahead a little. You know I still can't believe it that we are in South America and you have managed to surprise me." Michael looked at her sheepishly and put up his finger and asked, "May I say one more thing?"

Sarah looked at him indulgently and laughed. "You can say anything you want."

"Okay, just one more thing. I want you to know that the area of Patagonia is considered a plateau and is rainy most time of the year, but the most important detail is that the coast of Patagonia is the only place in the world where the Pacific and the Atlantic oceans meet. Ha, that's it. I think I finished for now."

"Thank you, kind sir. It was quite illuminating, and I shall try to contain all this information as we get to Patagonia because I am sure if I don't, my darling husband would remind me again."

"I am a real idiot. I know you know all these facts."

Sarah cut him short and said, "But you could not pass the opportunity to talk about it." She put her hands on his face and kissed him. She realized how much she loved her husband.

The most interesting factor about this area was the fact that it was the narrowest piece of land that separated the Atlantic from the Pacific.

Sarah was fascinated with his wide range of knowledge and realized that it had really been a childhood dream come true for him. Like anything else that Michael was interested in, he would explore it and check it out until he was satisfied with his findings.

Sarah asked, "Why didn't you ever suggest we visit this part of the world before?"

His answer was, "Sometimes I forget to turn my dreams into reality, and I am lucky enough to have you, my darling wife, to do it for me."

They flew from New York directly to Buenos Aires, which means "good air," the capital of Argentina. It is also called a small Europe in South America. It was a huge and magnificent city with a population of thirteen million people and many towering monuments and buildings. The multitude of warm colors of the houses, the street dancers, and the endless rhythm of Latin music engulfed them from everywhere. On every street corner or coffee bar there were local bands with very good musicians, and there were at least one or two couples dancing the famous tango with intricate and sensuous steps and variations.

On one street corner Sarah could see Michael wanted to dance, and although she was not an expert in Latin American dances, she proposed they join the local couples. And they did so to the applause of the small gathering of tourists and locals around them; however, after a few minutes a woman dressed in a tight-fitting and short red dress with high-heeled shoes tapped Sarah on her shoulder and claimed Michael as her partner. While the crowd cheered and clapped hands, the sensuous lady flew into Michael's arms, and they performed the tango to perfection.

Sarah was happy not to have to embarrass herself with the intricate steps, and Michael looked focused and thrilled at the same time. The crowd cheered them, and the band played a series of songs until Michael indicated he wished to stop. He kissed his partner on her cheeks and ordered a bottle of wine for her and the band.

From Buenos Aires they flew to San Carlos de Brioche, a quiet and beautiful Andean town with a population of 110,000, which doubles itself during tourist seasons. Brioche is surrounded with magnificent mountains and forests, and in winter it turns into a much-sought-after ski resort. In summer it is the destination for many active tourists who wish to engage in the many sports activities the area offers. They can go fishing, horse riding, hiking, and cycling.

To both their delight, Brioche is also Argentine's center of chocolate industry. The strong aroma of the chocolates lures people to the core of the manufacturing shops. The famous Miltre Avenue with its galleries and small boutiques of chocolatiers offers innocent tourists free samples and keeps them wanting more. Both Sarah and Michael were partial to good chocolate, and it was difficult to leave the area.

After tasting many flavors of chocolate, they took the number-twenty-two bus to the Swiss colony where they met Alfredo, a well-known expert on smoking meat. They watched him with wonder as he smoked big chunks of Argentine beef under hot sand and wood. Later they entered an inexpensive and traditionally hidden tavern where they ate small snacks of codfish and small bread balls infused with cheese called pão de queijo. The main course they ate consisted of tender Argentine prime beef and washed it all down with local beer.

From Brioche they took a bus to Perito Moreno near El Caliphate with its incredible sweet water potential and awesome landscapes. Then they crossed the border into Chile and went to Torus de Fina, the diamond spot of the Patagonia region and one of the finest wildlife reserves in the world. The area is rich with history, strong winds, dramatic landscapes, and colors. It is a paradise for nature lovers and hikers.

Their next destination was Ushuaia, and Michael told her it was the most southern city in the world and one thousand kilometers from Antarctica. Ushuaia is the capital of the province of Tierra del Fuego in Argentina and located along a wide bay.

It was lucky Sarah had the presence of mind to bring warm clothes and rainwear for both of them; however, they were still either cold or wet most of the time. They got on a boat and went to see the famous lighthouse at the "end of the world," about which Jules Vern had written. Their sea journey was exciting and cold at the same time. They watched the multitudes of penguins strutting along the beaches and the sleek seals lying on the rocks not far from the breathtaking sights of mighty glaciers.

After a restful night at a local hotel, they flew to the magnificent Iguassu Falls, which flow between Brazil and Argentina. They are amongst the most impressive water falls in the world. The double-border sites are packed daily with thousands of tourists from every corner of the world. There are many waterfalls, and they create a shimmering yet transparent panoramic wall of water and green trees. The sound of the falling waters is awesome, and the whole experience imprints itself on the mind.

Sarah knew that for the rest of their lives they would tell their children about the wonderful trip of their parents to South America.

Chapter 29

It was a bright and beautiful Saturday morning several months after they had returned from their most memorable holiday ever. Sarah was content to potter around the house and look through the piles of post on the table, and Michael was in his den, trying to catch up with all the urgent matters he had neglected to touch since their return home. He told Sarah that he didn't feel like ruining the sweet memories he had from their trip to Patagonia. "After all these months I feel as if I am still there with all the fascinating landscapes, smells, waterfalls, and fauna and you with me ... alone." She could see how much he had needed that break and decided to go away more often.

Laura and Arik had gone with Dora to an amusement park, and Tom and Dona were busy with each other in the garden. Sarah sat by the coffee table on the back porch and listened to soft music from the radio and sorted out the post in front of her. She was really happy to have gone with Michael on their trip. It was wonderful to be alone with him, to snuggle in bed without dreading any of the four children joining them or needing to solve a crisis at work. They had, however, told the children and the whole family in many details and at every opportunity about their amazing trip and showed photographs and memorabilia. The older twins promised to go there after they finished their studies, and the small ones shouted, "Ye, ye."

She could see from the corner of her eye that Tom was leaving his sister and going into the house to seek his father for some reason. It took only a minute for Dona to stand up and listen to something Sarah could not hear and then dash into the house after her brother. Suddenly it was Tom who came out and quietly asked Sarah to come with him. "Father is asleep, and he doesn't answer me." He told her with fear and despair in his eyes. Sarah sprang from her chair and dashed into the den, where she saw her twelve-year-old daughter holding her father's limp hand and crying. Michael was sitting next to the table, but his head was a little bent to the side. His glasses were on the table, and his eyes were open. There was a shade of a smile on his face as if he were thinking of something pleasant.

Sarah rushed to him and tried to find a pulse, but she immediately realized that Michael was no longer with them. She saw her two children, who were in a state of shock and disbelief, and knew it was her first duty to protect them. "Come, let's leave father alone and call for a doctor." She held both of them close to her body and exited the room.

"Tom, sweetheart, call both grandparents and just ask them to come over quickly and just say we need them. Dona, my love, I want you to be on the lookout for Dora and the small ones when they return so they won't go in to see father." Before she released them, she gave each one a big hug and said, "I need you, and I am very proud of you both."

Chapter 30
Older Sarah

Now so many years after Michael's death I remember once I had read in some ancient mythology that "man should not be too happy because the gods might become jealous."

Well, Michael's sudden death caught me unprepared for everything that waited for me. The fact that the children had found him before me put me into an automatic mode. I knew I had to take control of everything at once and look after the children's welfare first and then give in to my own grief and pain.

The moment I saw Michael's peaceful and inert face, I lost some part of my soul too, yet my body and mind kept functioning automatically and dealing with all that was necessary to be done in a situation like this.

With all the many matters that demanded my attention every second of the day, I put my deep feelings of shock and disbelief on hold and began attending to my four children's needs and to the grief of the elder generation. It broke my heart to watch Rachel and Jack absorbing the bitter news about their son and how hard they worked to support my children and be there for me too. Ben had arrived from London immediately after got the shocking news from his father. He shared his time between his parents and my children, who adored him. My brother, David, his wife, Mira, and their two grown-up children were constantly in and out of our house and did their best to distract my four children. My father and his wife simply left everything behind and tried to make it easier for all of us to bear the pain and grief we all shared.

I can't forget the horror in the eyes of Rachel and Jack once they realized what Tom had told them after they arrived to the house. The police had been present with the doctor, who pronounced Michael dead because of heart failure. Rachel simply collapsed onto the floor, and the two children went to help her get up. However, she was a trained nurse, and once she saw their grieving faces, she pulled herself up and didn't even let the doctor attend to her. She was a real trooper, and when I told her the children and I needed her, she contained her own grief and helped us all.

I was amazed to watch my children's reaction to the death of their adored father. Each of them had a special bond with Michael, and each of them kept alive a different trait or feature of Michael. Tom was growing up to become the spitting image of his father in his looks and stature. His hair was black, and a lock always covered his brows. He only had my gray eyes. Dona was quite tall for her age and had Michael's piercing deep blue eyes and his special brand of quiet humor. They both took after Michael and preferred the sciences and math studies over everything else. They had already practiced inventing things. They both became very successful when they grew older, though it took them months and years to get over Michael's sudden death.

Tom once said to me, "Dad didn't say good-bye before he left. I had so much to tell him and ask him and—"

"Yes, you are right. He didn't say good-bye, my love, but this is because he is always still with us and we can talk to him and tell him stuff."

He looked at me with his thoughtful gray eyes and said, "You know, Mum, I am surprised you say it because we are all talking to father." He saw the surprise in my eyes and continued, "Both Laura and Arik told Dona and me about their talks and laughs with father." He looked at me to see if I believed him and continued, "It is true that Dona and I talk to him too, but I never asked him about why he left so suddenly. I thought it wasn't polite."

I was amazed at the wisdom of my child and hugged him to me for a long time. I thought it would be right to tell them the real reason why their father left us all so suddenly, so in one of our family gatherings I told them about his heart failure.

"The doctor told me he found father had a congenital defect in his heart, which had never been detected. What happened is that the flow of oxygen-rich blood to a section of his heart muscle suddenly became blocked and the heart didn't get any oxygen, and that caused the death of the heart muscles." I stopped to see whether they had comprehended all the details and then continued, "The doctor promised me that it was instantaneous and he didn't feel any pain." I made a little prayer they would soon forget about it.

It had become a family tradition with the children and the close family and friends to hold a memorial for Michael once a year. We would first attend the grave, and the children would prepare a poem or bring one of their school projects to show Michael and tell him about. We would all say a personal silent prayer, and each year we would do something else. We would go on family picnics in the countryside or go on hikes to sites Michael liked.

One time we showed a film from our trip to South America to the whole family, and I had to tell them small anecdotes from the trip. It was amazing how alive and wonderful Michael looked, and it extracted varied reactions from the people present. The children and Michael's parents cried openly, and sometimes I thought either I would choke on my tears or my heart would burst with love and craving for him.

Some other times we all went to the plant where the employees displayed new and advanced inventions produced by the firm or later by the older children who had joined the film. This tradition had become an annual bonding date for the children and grandparents, and we all made the utmost effort to attend it.

The little ones were too young at the time, but they missed their father so much that sometimes I could not contain the compassion and sorrow I felt for their personal loss. It was amazing to watch how the older children told the younger ones about their father. There was a five-year gap between the two twins, yet Tom and Dona never ceased to tell them about what they had managed to do with Michael, the places they had gone with him, and what he had taught them before the younger ones were born.

The uncanny bond between Tom and Dona existed between Laura and Arik too. Many years later I once asked Dona why she rushed from the garden after Tom had gone into the house. She looked at me and simply said, "He called me to come." And when I asked Tom if he had called her, he smiled and said, "Mummy, I don't have to call her. She simply knows when I need her."

My period of mourning began long after everybody else who loved and cared for Michael had adapted to his lose. I loved Michael for all the normal reasons like his commitment to the children; his generosity, his brilliant mind, his wisdom, and his love for the children and me, but there was more. He was a wonderful lover and partner till our last day together. He was bright and inventive. He was generous and loyal to a fault and a great father. He was extremely handsome and a great dancer. However, I think what kept us so happy together was the fact that the initial love and trust we felt for each other was dynamic and gained different facets and different configuration each day of our marriage.

I believe that if love is not dynamic and doesn't change with you, it can sometime turn stale. Love should constantly be nourished if it is expected to stay fresh and meaningful. One has to expect love to change and one should change with it. Otherwise it is doomed to die or fail you.

Chapter 31

Young Sarah

Sarah was nearly thirty-nine years old when she became a widow with four young children and owned a very prosperous and advanced electronics firm. It dawned on her that Michael must have thought about the possibility of his early demise when he asked her to join him in the firm. She believed he might have had some kind of premonition about what was to come and recalled his unusual bequest to her before they got married. She only regretted he never shared his premonitions with her. After she had read his last will and testimony, she found out that he had left her all his worldly goods and money, including his shares in his companies, in the house and in some new ongoing ventures.

Sarah understood she was considered a woman of substantial means, but it didn't mean much to her, as her beloved husband was not there with her to share it. She missed Michael and his love for her. She missed loving him and sharing the joys and sorrows of raising the children together. She missed his physical proximity everywhere. She craved his touch, his body scent, the feeling of his skin when she caressed him, and most of all she missed their lovemaking and moments of intimacy.

Life engulfed Sarah from every direction. She shared her time mainly between the office and her home. As she knew most of the aspects of Michael's work, she decided to employ an experienced engineer to help her deal with the technical side of the work while she dealt mainly with the marketing and advertising side of it. Michael had built a professional and very loyal team in his different concerns, and the work flowed smoothly. When there was any crisis, it was brought to the attention of the board, and with the help of Jack, Sarah resolved them.

At home Dora had a new boyfriend named Nisso, who was a gardener and who had convinced Dora he would look after her forever. Nisso was much older than Dora and didn't want any children of his own. Dora was happy with him, and they both had become indispensable to the whole family and shared the load with Sarah. Dora took care of the everyday chores of the household, and when there was need, she got someone to help her. Sarah was left with the office work and the overwhelming task of the children's education without the comforting presence and help of Michael.

She couldn't believe how much she had relied on Michael with the children and the fact that they talked and shared their thoughts. They had created an ongoing flow of information between them. She remembered how Michael would recall his own experience with his younger brother and how they were solved. He told her about what he wanted each child to have in addition to his genetic heritage. He often spoke about values, such as creativity, curiosity, and decency at work and at home.

It was important to him that each child would have his or her own individual inner voice, and it was the duty of parents to nourish their children's hidden dreams and needs. She knew she had had a fine man for a husband and made sure she followed in light of his dreams when she was dealing with the children.

All five of them had a weekly family council when they discussed any issues or problems that had occurred during the week. It was a sacred time for all of them, and they had all benefitted from it for years. Sarah knew that she had to keep focused on the children and the office if she didn't want to fall apart.

Her father was her best ally. She realized he had long experience with being alone after her mother had passed away and left him to take care of David and her. She told her father how much she missed her mother all the time and he simply wrapped her in his arms and let their deep sadness wash away from them.

Joe took Sarah out to concerts and the theater and quite often joined her on her daily swims in the sea. He also accompanied her abroad when she had to meet with Michael's clients or close deals with them. He had sold his own company and had partially retired from any work apart from helping Sarah. They would go to exhibitions and restaurants as they used to do when she was young and lived at home with him. Ruth would often join them, but she knew it was quality time and healing time for both of them.

Once during a flight to New York Sarah happened to mention Michael and how much he liked to dance. She had that wistful look in her eyes. "You know, Dad, I miss Michael in thousand ways each day and night despite the many years that have passed, but I miss him most when he would do things out of the ordinary, when he would behave as if there was no tomorrow. He loved to dance with me and the children without any apparent reason. He would come behind me in the kitchen while I would be preparing food and say, 'They are playing our music, so let's dance.' It could be Nat King Cole, a Vienna waltz, or a fast tango. He would whirl me around the house or the lawn. Then the children would join, and he would dance with them until we would all fall down and giggle like mad."

She was quiet for some time, lost in her memories, but then her father caught both her hands in his and looked tenderly into her sparkling eyes. "Listen to me, Sarah. You know I miss Michael very much. I had come to love him not only because of his love and devotion to you and the children but especially for himself. He was a fine man, and I wish he were here instead of me. But you, Sarah, are still young, only forty-five years old, and you have your whole future ahead of you.

It has been more than five years since Michael died, and you have not dated anyone seriously. I know for a fact that many good men have tried to date you, but you always say you are not ready. I know it has been hard on you and the kids and you might be thinking about me and your mum, but it is different with you."

She turned to look at him with tears in her eyes "How different? You didn't date any woman seriously for at least ten years after mother had died from cancer. What is different? I still love Michael and miss him with every bone and fiber of my body. How can I accept anybody else into my heart and my children's hearts?"

"Sweetheart, just try. Open your heart to the possibility of meeting someone else that might not take Michael's place in your heart but would be there alongside Michael. You need him not only for the kids, who need the presence of a male figure in their life, but especially for yourself."

"You mean to say I deprive my children of something because of their dead father? They have me anytime of the day or the night. They have Dora and Nisso 24-7, and both you and Ruth and Rachel and Jack are constantly at the house. The children both love you all and depend on you. I don't feel ready to bring a stranger into our home just because I have to fill it with a male presence."

Her father knew Sarah well enough not to push the point. He knew from Rachel, Michael's mother, who had also spoken to Sarah about the same issue and had urged her to look for a new mate. It seemed that although Sarah was very adamant in her views, but finally she said, "Okay, Dad, I know you are all worried about me, and I promise to think about it more."

"My dear, I am always here for you and the children, but I would like to see you happy again." She remained silent and kept looking out of the plane window with a faraway look in her eyes.

Chapter 32

The children grew up, and the years passed. Both Tom and Dona were about to go to college and begin their separate life from home. Long before they graduated from high school, Sarah had asked them both to join her at the firm and begin their acquaintance with the work being done there. They both showed strong tendencies toward computers, math, and electronics, so it was quite natural for them to be curious about their family firm and wish to be part of it. It was important for Sarah to keep them involved with their father's work and carry on with it in the future.

The younger twins seemed to go in a different direction completely. Arik wanted to become an actor. He loved music and all the performing arts, and Laura had always showed great talent in painting and sculpting, so it was clear she would gravitate toward the visual arts.

Sarah's father had often urged her to go out on dates, but she didn't seem to consider the idea earnestly. She had a lot of offers from prominent and attractive suitors in the business world and the academy in addition to writers, artists, and politicians, but from the start she felt she couldn't stick it out with any of them. After many tries and dates, she realized she simply wasn't ready to bond with anybody new and decided to avoid the issue and expected everybody to respect her wishes.

Chapter 33

On one of her frequent flights to Berlin to meet the German partners, she decided to take a short detour and fly to Paris first. It was a preferred destination for her and Michael. They had often flown there for short weekends and loved the special ambiance of the city; its boulevards, the riverbank, and its magnificent architecture, and in particular they loved to wine and dine there.

Sara normally flew first-class and preferred to either sleep during the flight with an eyeshade or just read and do some work. She hardly ever conversed with anybody, and she cherished her privacy. She noticed the flight was late and the crew seemed to be waiting for a passenger. It took ten more minutes before the doors were shut and the plane began to roll toward takeoff. Sarah was looking out of the window when she felt someone sit down on the next seat near her. He didn't say anything and just fastened his seatbelt and made himself comfortable. The flight attendants began dispensing drinks and seeing to the comfort of the few passengers in the first-class cabin. Sarah asked for gin, tonic, ice, and lemon and continued looking out of the porthole as the plane took off.

In Sarah's opinion takeoff was the most crucial stage of the whole flight, and she always seemed to get tense. She wasn't aware of the flight attendant offering her a drink, and she seemed to be holding her breath. Suddenly she heard the passenger next to her talking to her, and she turned to look and saw the worried faces of the flight attendant and the late-coming passenger looking at her. She released her breath and smiled sheepishly. "I don't like takeoffs," she said and accepted the drink willingly.

"I, too, hate takeoffs. I am always afraid the plane is too heavy for the engines and we might not stay airborne." The man next to her took a sip of his whiskey and smiled at her.

Sarah was grateful to him for being considerate and placing himself in the same situation as her. She looked at him more closely and saw an urban-looking man wearing a beautifully tailored Italian dark blue suit with very fine gray stripes. His shirt was light blue, and his tie was ... a Dior silk tie. She recognized it at once because she had bought several of them for Michael. She looked at his face and suddenly felt a jolt. His hair was still curly; however, it was trendily cut, and his black eyes were focused on her.

Sarah remembered his deep baritone voice and was mortified. It was Alex, her student from university, from the stains on the silk blouse, from the shameful incident so many years before.

It was obvious that Alex had recognized her earlier, and now he simply smiled at her pleasantly and tried to make her feel comfortable.

"It is you, Alex, aren't you?" She looked at him expectantly, and he just nodded his head.

"Sorry, *mea culpa*. I am guilty."

She was mortally embarrassed and blushed like a teenager. "I am mortified, and I owe you an apology. I only discovered my indiscretion after you had left the lesson. I apologize, although it is more than fifteen years too late."

"I am sorry if I caused you any inconvenience then, but I really didn't know what to do." He looked embarrassed too.

"You see, at the time I was not married and had no experience with nursing mothers."

Sarah looked into his eyes and realized he was sincere. She turned her head and looked out through the window at the blue skies and tried to recover her poise. "Thank you for being so understanding."

He shrugged his shoulders a little and just smiled.

"It has been so long and so much has happened to both of us, right?" She looked at him with surprise, and he just nodded his head. He noticed she had gulped down her drink, so he ordered another round from the flight attendant.

"Were you the passenger the plane was waiting for?" she asked.

Once again he said, "*Mea culpa*. Guilty as charged." He didn't add any other explanation, and Sarah knew not to ask anything if the other person didn't divulge it himself.

They got their drinks, and Sarah declined the attendant's offer to have something to eat. "I am fine. Thank you." Alex declined the offer too.

Sarah was surprised to realize she was excited and relaxed at the same time. There was something about Alex as a man that excited her, and at the same time she felt relaxed. He attracted her like no man had done so for years. She had not been curious or drawn to anybody since Michael had died, and although it felt strange, she was happy about it.

"Are you going to Paris on business or pleasure?" she asked in a casual voice.

Alex looked at her thoughtfully and said, "I am going for pleasure. I am on my way to Berlin, but I thought it would be nice to spend a couple of days in this lovely city." He paused and then continued, "You might think I am vain or mad, but I like to do some of my shopping in Paris." He shrugged his shoulders again like the French do and just smiled.

Sarah looked at him aghast. "I am going to Paris for the same reason and for the city itself. I am also flying to Berlin after a couple of days on business." She stopped for a minute and then carried on, "I can't believe it. What a coincidence, don't you think?"

He just nodded his head and continued drinking his whiskey. It seemed they were staying not far from each other but in different hotels in the elegant section of the city.

"Are you afraid of landings too?" he asked her with a soft smile, and she said it was less stressing than the takeoff.

"So if you are not already busy, would you care to have dinner with me this evening?"

She sensed that although he was composed and calm, he was holding his breath. He wasn't sure about her answer. She smiled at him and said, "It would be my pleasure to dine with you this evening. It is the first time that I have been invited to dinner by a student of mine."

She immediately realized she had made a mistake. She could see he didn't like the tag she had attached to him. "I apologize for my poor wording. I didn't mean it that way." She touched his hand briefly and continued, "I can see from how you look and sound that you have not been a student for many years, and I am not your tutor. *Mea culpa*. This time I am guilty of bad manners. Are we still okay for dinner tonight?" She looked truly contrite, and Alex couldn't refuse her sincere apology.

"I shall pick you up at seven from your hotel. Do you have any preference in terms of food?"

She smiled and said, "I simply like French food. All the rest is less important."

He came to collect her just on time and was dressed impeccably. His dark blue jacket and pale yellow shirt went perfectly with his tan trousers. He wore a new tie with fine willow tree leaves in green, yellow, and matching tan dots. It was another Dior silk tie. Alex noticed her looking at it and said, "Is there something wrong with my ties?"

"Of course not; I am simply surprised because I realize they are silk Dior ties, and I used to buy them for my husband. In fact, they are my favorites."

"Good." His eyes went over her entire attire appreciatively. He appreciated the lovely off-white Chanel suit, the diamonds on her wrist and ears, and the high-heeled black pumps, and he savored a whiff of her perfume. His eyes rested on her strands of auburn hair and then slid to her bosom, "You look as beautiful as ever if I may say it."

Sarah smiled graciously.

Alex was attentive, knowledgeable, funny, and dashing. The wine and the food were excellent; however, what excited her most was the conversation they had. He hardly spoke about himself and didn't ask her any personal questions. He seemed to be content with what she chose to tell him and what he already guessed about her four children and the company she owned. He told her he was divorced, that he had two teenage daughters, and that he traveled a lot.

Most of the conversation was about world affairs, art exhibitions, the theater, and the kind of music he loved most, namely operas. "I must confess my mother was a singer in Russia, and we all loved classical music. Would you like to go with me to the ballet and see *Swan Lake* by Tchaikovsky in the famous Paris opera house tomorrow night?"

Sarah was thrilled. "I have not been there for years, and I remember the colorful Chagall ceiling. Thank you."

She recalled the fabulous evening she and Michael had spent in town but refrained from mentioning it. "Won't it be difficult to get tickets for tomorrow night?'

She looked at him inquiringly, but he put her mind at ease. "Don't worry. I have a friend who works in the ticket office of the opera, and I know they always reserve some good tickets for emergencies." He smiled impishly and continued, "We are an emergency."

They walked along the Seine River and tried to identify famous monuments and buildings. They stopped at small bars and drank some local wine, and Sarah felt a little tipsy; however, she also felt young and desirable again with all the hot, furtive glances Alex was sending in her direction.

She knew he was excited and attracted to her and at one point he took her hand in his and kept her close to his lean body. It was a wonderful sensation to feel a man's body attached to hers. He looked vigorous and very athletic. He walked to her hotel, and just before she went in, he turned her in his arms, looked at her smiling eye, and kissed her lightly on her lips. "I am coming to take you shopping tomorrow, so don't go anywhere without me."

Chapter 34

It was a lovely, bright day, and Alex had prepared many attractions for her. They went into small boutiques and studios. They looked at current art trends and fashions. They sat in street corner cafes for drinks and coffee and looked at the passersby, and then they ate a light lunch in the fabulous lobby of the Hôtel George V. Everywhere they went, people seemed to know Alex and were ready to serve him and his *très jolie* companion. Sarah had learned to speak French at school and felt comfortable with the language, but Alex spoke fluently. He told her that at his home they spoke French as well as Russian, and Sarah knew that French people always appreciated foreigners who could speak their language.

At gallery La Fayette he wanted to buy her a small bottle of perfume. "I know you like the scent of Dior. I can smell it on you."

But she refused. "I like to buy my own cosmetics, but thanks anyway." She didn't know why she refused his well-meant offer, but it didn't appeal to her. He seemed to be surprised by her reaction, but he chose to let it go.

On the whole Sarah was impressed and flattered. It was good to go out with a man who knew his way around one of the most beautiful and most fashionable cities in the world. He attended to all her needs and catered to all her wishes. He seemed to know in an uncanny way what she desired and when she was tired or bored. At one point she said to him, "You seem to know so much about me."

He smiled at her roguishly and asked, "Does the lady have any complaint about the service?"

She just nodded her head in wonder.

They managed to get to the Dorsey Museum to see the current Monet water lilies exhibition and then rushed to their respective hotels. Sarah was exhilarated and excited as she had not been for many years. She loved Paris's promise of surprises and pleasure.

She put on a black satin dress that emphasized her lovely figure and wore Michael's diamond necklace with the matching drop earrings. Her hair was put up with an intricate art deco-style clasp. Sarah was most pleased with her latest acquisition. She had bought a new pair of red shoes in a small boutique in the Latin Quarter, and on her shoulders she wore a red satin jacket that molded around her figure.

Alex was duly impressed and gave one long whistle when he got to the hotel lobby.

"You are gorgeous and amazing. Who would believe you have four children with this figure of yours?" Sarah was pleased and complimented him on his light gray Italian suit, mauve shirt, and a multiple color silk tie. He looked as if he had walked out of a man's journal.

"Where did you learn how to dress up so elegantly?" she wondered.

After a short pause he said, "I simply can afford it now. I couldn't before."

She looked at him appreciatively and uttered, "Well, you sure know what you are doing."

He gave a small bow and said, "Thank you, dear princess, anything to please you." Sarah thought there was a hint of irony in his words. Then he grabbed her by her arm, and they left for the opera.

It was a gala performance of *Swan Lake* and a total triumph. The ballet company itself was from Kiev with the French Philharmonic Orchestra. Tchaikovsky's music was beautifully lyrical, and one was totally carried away with the tragic story and the ethereal performance of the dancers. The whole evening was a lovely experience. The opera house itself, which is located in the center of Paris, is a magnificent building from the outside, and once you get in, it engulfs you with its rich décor, incredible paintings, and architecture. The magnificent Chagall figures on the ceiling are a unique focus of attention.

Sarah was overwhelmed with the whole experience and the special ambiance of the evening. There were many tourists like themselves among the audience; however, a major part consisted of local Parisians, many of whom were young people. Many ladies wore long evening gowns, and the men were in formal attire.

Alex seemed to be excited too, and he held her hand throughout the performance. Sarah found it endearing and gave a small squeeze to his hand. A taxi took them to a small bistro, and they had a delicious French meal with excellent wine. Sarah could feel the wine and the warm food casting their effect on her. She didn't have time to rest during the day, and it was all catching up with her. Alex was attentive and amusing, but at times he seemed as if he would devour her with his eyes; however, he continued behaving as a perfect gentleman.

At one stage he bent toward her and said, "It all seems like a dream come true being here with you in Paris and enjoying an evening together."

"What do you mean by a dream come true?" She was puzzled. "Did you think about me all these years and have fantasies?" she asked incredulously.

He laughed. "Are you kidding? We all had fantasies about you. You were the idol of all the male students' wet dreams in the faculty. We all thought you were the hottest chick on the campus, what with your looks and your rich, brilliant husband." He paused for a moment and then continued, "But you were also untouchable."

Sarah was stunned. She had never imagined she could possibly play the role of sex symbol to her students. What Alex had just told her shed a completely different light on her own image as a serious university faculty member. Michael never hinted to her that there was anything wrong or improper in her behavior or appearance.

She saw Alex was uncomfortable with what he had said and tried to change the subject. "I am sorry if I have offended you, but all of us really admired you because of your sharp mind and because you were unlike any of the female professors or students in the math faculty ... or for that matter, in any of the technology or science departments." He stretched his hands toward her in a plea. "It was meant as a compliment, believe me."

Sarah relaxed and drank some of her water.

Alex looked at her seriously and said, "I am sorry to have ruined this wonderful evening for you, and if I could take it all back, I would. Could you forgive me?"

He really looked sorry and miserable about the incident. Sarah stretched her hands toward him and caught his. "Don't worry. You see, I am having a wonderful time with you. The ballet was incredible, and the food is delicious. I am really very happy to be here in Paris with you. I still can't believe it that we met just like that after so many years and you love Paris as much as I do." She squeezed his hand and sat back.

He looked at her eyes for a minute and realized she was sincere. "I can see you are tired and would like to return to your hotel."

"Yes, thank you. It was a wonderful day, and tomorrow I am flying to Berlin."

"So am I," he said quietly.

Sarah could feel Alex regretted what he had told her. She felt sorry for him because he was such wonderful company and so sexy. They were equally attracted to each other, and she just needed some respite from life. Alex paid the bill, and while he was putting Sarah's red jacket on her shoulders, he kissed her neck and inhaled her scent. "I am sorry, you know?" He looked at her so sheepishly that she laughed and turned around in his arms and kissed him on his lips.

"Don't get carried away with your dreams, okay?" she warned him.

They walked into the hotel lobby embracing each other and laughing, and although she was a bit apprehensive about the outcome of the evening, Sarah was excited.

Alex made her feel vibrant and alive, and she felt desired. There was an elusive quality about Alex she couldn't put a name to; however, he intrigued her, and she felt like a woman again. They reached her door, and he held her tight in his arms and whispered into her hair, "May I stay with you tonight?" She lifted her head and looked into his smoldering eyes, and he continued, "I want to make love to you very much." He nestled his face in her mass of long hair, which was spread all around her shoulders and back, and inhaled her scent hungrily. She led him into her room and didn't turn on the lights.

Alex was an expert lover. At first he just held her in his arms and showered her face and head with small little kisses. From the start Sarah was acutely aware of his manhood, which prodded against her pelvis while he ignited the fire of passion in her whole body. He slowly took off her clothes piece by piece as if it were a ritual. He examined her long, trim figure and touched every limb with his hands and tongue. Sarah was amazed by his total absorption in what he was doing. He seemed to be memorizing every inch of her body and enjoying it like a child. "You are beautiful and just perfect." He mumbled to himself all the time and Sarah felt like laughing.

When she stood completely naked in front of him, she said, "It's your turn now, buster, so stand still and let me see how you look." She was pleased with his strong, tapered body and what attracted her eyes most was his manhood. It seemed to have a life of its own. It stretched erect forward and seemed to communicate something to her. Sarah smiled and took it in her hands and attached her own supple body to his. Alex went mad.

He carried her to the bed and lay on top of her while his hands molded her breasts and then sucked each nipple hungrily. He passed his hands on her buttocks, her thighs, her arms, and her face. Sarah held to him and put her fingers in his thick, curly black hair and pulled his face down for her to kiss. He bit her lips and then caught her tongue and fenced with it. He then left her face, and his tongue began its slow descent along her body until it reached her center. Sarah was roused and eager, but he took his time to explore her inner sex with his tongue and his deft fingers. Sarah moaned with pleasure and opened her thighs to his probing while she held him close to her body with her legs.

Sarah felt his strong, pulsing sex digging into her pelvis and sought release from the tension building up inside her for so long. She held his manhood in her hands and after considering its weight and caressing it with her fingers, she brought it to the core of her desire. Alex was tuned into her needs and pushed himself into her wet cavity and began thrusting in and out in frenzy. Suddenly his body convulsed, and he felt a molted stream of fire gushing out of him and into Sarah. He cried, "Oh, god. Oh, god," several times and then collapsed on her. Sarah exploded too and felt how her inner organs were melting with the sense of what had happened.

Alex's laborious breathing subsided after a while, and he lifted his body on his elbows and looked at Sarah's flushed face and sparkling eyes. "You don't know what it means to me. You can't imagine. Thank you." She smiled and gave him a peck on his lips. She disengaged herself form their tangled bodies and rested her head on his chest. She listened to her body and felt her blood flow through her limbs. It had been a long time, and she had needed it.

Alex lay beside her, his arms embracing her body, lost in his thoughts. She turned her head and asked him, "Are you okay?" He leaned on one arm and perused her face for telltales.

"I am more than fine. I feel more than just wonderful, but I want to apologize for not waiting for you to finish. I simply had to come. Otherwise I knew I would explode." He paused and then continued, "I don't think you want to hear why."

Sarah noticed his whole body was trembling a bit, and she gathered him to herself and held him tightly. "How long has it been since you were last with a woman, if I may query?" she asked softly.

"It is not that. It is you."

"What do you mean it is me?" she asked, and he seemed reluctant to talk about it and just bent to kiss her lips.

Suddenly she was bothered by something. She wondered why he had not said a word to her about being late for the flight to Paris. He saw her pensive face and asked, "What is bothering you, my pretty woman?"

"I wonder why you had to hold the plane before takeoff. Are you a government agent, or is that top secret?"

She could see she had hit on a nerve given how he pondered in his mind whether to tell her or not.

"I am normally not inquisitive," she added, "and if it is a secret, then don't tell me, but seriously what was so urgent?"

It took him a long while before he answered her. Sarah was almost sure he was a government agent and couldn't disclose its nature or blow his cover, but he did seem to have a serious debate within himself. She thought back about all their talks and realized he had never said anything about what he did for a living and what had happened to him after he had finished his studies. Just before she decided to let him off the hook, he said, "It is difficult for me to talk about it, and you might not like it. But I don't want this to be between us." He looked somber, and there were small drops of perspiration on his brow. "You see, I held the flight because of you."

"What are you talking about? What has holding up the flight got to do with me?"

"In order to answer your question properly, I'd better begin with the last time we spoke. I hope you remember you sent me a note saying my solution to the problem you presented in class was ingenious and new to you. You congratulated me on my ingenuity, and it pleased me a lot. By the way, I still keep your note at home." He paused a little and looked preoccupied with his journey along memory lane. He lifted his face and focused on her eyes and continued with his bewildering monologue.

"You see, Sarah, although you had not seen me after that encounter, I did see you. I followed your life with all its major events—the birth of your two twins, your husband's meteoric success, your trips abroad." He saw her flinch with this piece of information, but he continued in a monotonous voice. "Yes, I know all about your trip to Patagonia and the Iguassu Falls and how much you both enjoyed it, about Tom's bicycle accident, and about Michael's love for you."

Sarah lay aghast beside him. She slowly pulled away from him and felt how her body was curling into a fetal position. Alex was aware of her movements, but he seemed not to bother about it.

"So you knew I was on that flight to Paris? How could you do it?"

He didn't flinch or apologize for the pain and anger expressed in her voice but resumed his sordid little story in the same flat tone. "After my graduation I was accepted to MIT and finished my PhD at the top of my class there; however, I came home as often as I could, and I always had someone monitoring your life for me." He paused again but didn't look at her. He just stretched on his back and quietly rendered the story of his appalling infatuation with her.

"You are right. I do work for the government in a very special capacity, so it is not difficult for me to take any flight I wish anywhere in the world. When I found out that you were flying to Paris and Berlin alone for a change, I knew I had the best opportunity to meet you 'accidentally.' I put on hold all my affairs in the office and asked my secretary to fix my flights, the seats, the ballet, the lot." He cast a quick glance at her stony face and continued, "I didn't have any compunction about holding the flight for fifteen minutes. The captain promised me he could make up for the delay during the flight." He tried to take Sarah's hand; however, she moved back, and he smiled at her sadly.

"*Mea culpa.* I am gravely guilty from the look I see in your eyes. I want you to know I am not proud of my behavior, but I am not ashamed either. I have been in love with you ever since the first day you walked into class with your magnificent figure and aura of an untouchable princess. I couldn't stand up in class because I had a continuous hard-on. It was impossible for me to stand or walk in front of you or even look you in the eyes. I suppose it all sounds quite sordid to you now, but that is the reason behind everything I have done concerning you.

Sarah kept quiet and thought about how puzzled she had been with the coincidence of their meeting, with his Christian Dior ties and tailored cloths. Michael always wore tailored suits when he traveled abroad on business and on official occasions, and Sarah bought him the finest shirts and ties. She felt used and tainted and refrained from looking at Alex.

Sarah covered her naked body with a blanket and went to sit on the edge of the bed with her back to him.

"I can see from your body language that I shouldn't have told you all this, but I couldn't deceive you anymore. It is quite clear to me that what I want and what I need from you cannot exist on a basis of deception and secrets. I would have liked you to be a full partner in my life now that you are a widow. I can give you anything, even children if you wish, but I do not think you would consider such a possibility now. I want you to know that I have truly loved you for all these years, but I realize now that my love for you wasn't justification enough to permit me to invade your privacy so flagrantly. And for that I am sorry." He gave her a self-deprecating smile and went quiet.

"Would you like to ask me anything before I leave?" His voice was devoid of all emotion, and he seemed to have reconciled himself to the grim outcome of their short affair.

Sarah had her hands wrapped around her body and considered his question. She didn't turn to look at him but asked in a small voice. "I can't understand why did you do it and why for so long."

He considered her question for few minutes and then said, "Now that I look back on all these years and efforts I devoted to following your life from afar, I don't have any logical reason to give. Loving you or being infatuated with you should not have gone so far. It shouldn't have become the obsession it had become." He paused and then continued, "I know a million little details about your life and your habits, but somehow I missed getting to know your moral preferences and inner core."

Sarah got off the bed and stood up erect, looking him straight in the eyes, and then she said, "Thank you for being honest with me at last. I believe it wasn't easy for you to come clean after all these years, and I appreciate it. There is nothing I would like to say. So I am going into the bathroom now, and I would be grateful if you were to leave before I come out."

He stood on the other side of the bed with his head bent in acceptance of her decision.

"Thank you for your gracious reaction. I know I don't deserve it; however, I promise I would not follow you to Berlin tomorrow. I also promise never again to stalk you or your family in any way."

"Thank you, Alex, and—" she said, and after a short pause she added, "Be happy."

Chapter 35

Older Sarah

The long summer days are nearly over, and I can feel the early chill of fall in the mornings, especially because I am living so close to the sea. There is something comforting for me, and I expect most people of my generation to live this phase of life in a familiar ambiance and surrounded by the same comfortable objects and environment of our childhood. Many of my friends have gone to live in special homes either willingly, or they have been urged into it by their families; however, I am very comfortable in my parents' old home by the sea and wouldn't change it for any palace.

Even before I open my eyes, I know the morning mist is covering the surface of the sea like a thick blanket, and small vapors are coming into my bedroom. It is the time Ariel usually visits me, and I am excited. I love the way he entices me into the mode of being alive and pampered.

I can feel Ariel's presence in my room now. He is among the soft vapors that enter the room. This morning he just wrapped his amorphous wings around my body and softly smoothed all the folds and wrinkles on my skin away. It always amazes me how although I can't touch him, I can sense his ethereal weight on my flesh.

"It was time Alex came back and went out of your life forever," he whispered into my inner ear, and I knew he was following my stream of thoughts and memories of Alex when I last met him in Paris.

After Alex had left my room in the hotel, I took a long, hot shower and tried to rid myself of the unpleasant residue his sordid presence and monologue had left behind. I was not angry with Alex. Nor did I feel as if he used me sexually. He was a lovely lover, and I had enjoyed his company and the sex we had until he began with his unpleasant revelations. What did upset me was his long habit of stalking me and my family. It was a gross intrusion into our lives, and I resented it very much. I always cherished the memory of the trip Michael and I took to South America, and the fact that Alex knew all about it galled me. I knew there wasn't anything sinister in what he had done, yet there was subterfuge and deceit in his actions.

My trip to Berlin was almost eventless. I met our partners, signed some papers about a joint future merger between us, and went to a beautiful concert with Christian and his wife with the Berlin Philharmonic Orchestra. The flight back home to my family and work took off on time.

When they were young, my children were my daily concern and responsibility. With the help of Dora and the rest of the family, I had to look after their welfare and cater for their food, clothes, and studies on a daily basis; however, now that Tom and Dona are out of the house most part of the weekdays and Laura and Arik are busy with their many school activities and studies, my meetings with them take a new and different dimension.

The older twins are totally engrossed in their university studies, friends, and experiments at their father's plant, but they always find time to go out with me to restaurants, buy me tickets to some fringe shows we all like, or simply talk to me about the news or their current loves. I am extremely proud of their sensitivity to my needs and how they endeavor to continue the serenity of our life as if Michael were alive.

Suddenly they have become my friends and partners, and I consult with them in matters concerning the plant, any changes I wish to make in the house, or matters concerning the young twins.

The uncanny bond they all had since childhood never ceased. All four are good friends, and I can trust them to look out for one another at all times. The younger twins try to follow their elder brothers' example, and every week we would still meet even if only the three of us could spend some quality time together. I always thank Michael in my heart for giving me such wonderful children.

I think that sex and the possibility of deriving any pleasure from sensual and erotic activities begin in the mind.

"It is all in the mind." That is what Michael used to say, and after one look at me, he would suggest we stop everything and take a break. He would always finish it by saying, "I can't do anything when my mind is elsewhere."

I am not talking about the beastly satisfaction that comes from acts of rape or using force and causing pain. Gross pornography and all kinds of child abuse are detestable and abhorrent in my mind too.

When I met Alex on the plane to Paris, I had been celibate for many years. During those years I had dated many guys, but I had never found any single one attractive enough for either engage in sex or anything else. I simply couldn't mentally or emotionally bond with any of them. My mind and body never showed signs of being attracted to anyone. I suppose the attraction stemmed from our first encounter when I met Alex at university. There had been some kind of attraction between us. At the time I was happily married to Michael, and Alex was my student; however, when I met him on the plane, there were no barriers between us, and I felt happy to have met him.

I finally understand why I dwell on my short affair with Alex, and I realize that although we were attracted to each other and physically compatible, we were poles apart when it came to moral compatibility. I suppose that is as critical and important for any bond to exist between couples.

Chapter 36

Young Sarah

Sarah had just returned from a long trip to New York and was happy to be back home. It had been almost ten years since her memorable trip to South America with Michael. She was happy to note that she was right not to worry about any further contact from Alex. It had been four years since she met him on the plane to Berlin and found out about his obsession with her and his stalking of her family. He seemed to have disappeared into thin air, and she gave a sigh of relief.

It was late in the afternoon, and the heat of the summer urged her to go swimming in the sea. She had kept her small house annexed to the family home in her name because the children used to go there from time to time when they wanted to visit her father or be on their own. Her father and Ruth had left the villa and gone to live in a modern, high-rise apartment building in the city where all their friends were. Sarah used her annexed part as a refuge too and often rested on the porch after her long swims.

Standing outside and looking at the expanse of silver blue water in front of her, she spotted someone on her rock. She knew her father was away, and it was very unusual to find any stranger swim to the rock and lay there. She became curious and kept looking, trying to identify his identity. Suddenly he began waving to her, and she missed a heartbeat. It reminded her of someone from the far past. She guessed she knew the figure but couldn't put a name to it. The sun was in her eyes, and it was too far.

The figure got into the water and began swimming toward shore while she walked down the stone steps leading to the beach. The man reached the beach and stood up on the sand, dripping with water.

He was still slim and tall, and his light brown eyes sparkled with joy when she came closer. He opened his arms to her, and she ran into them with a carefree sprint of a young girl.

"Ethan, it is you, my Ethan, right?" she asked incredulously and wrapped her arms around him and put her head on his shoulder, a big sigh escaping her body. He stood still and simply absorbed the impact of her exhilarating presence in his arms.

"I know it is you, Sarah. It can only be you," he said softly.

They held each other for a long time until Sarah became self-conscious of her proximity to Ethan's half-naked body, and he became aware of the water dripping from his hair and face onto Sarah's clothes.

She still had the figure of a Nordic Amazon, and the scent of her glorious chestnut hair still filled his nostril with fierce longing for this woman. He tried to disengage himself from her body, but her face was buried in his chest. When she lifted her head at last, her beautiful gray eyes were sparkling with tears.

"I can't tell you how happy I am to see you." She looked into his warm brown eyes and began walking beside him toward the house.

"I am camping in your father's house," he told Sarah. "I told him I wanted to visit you, and he suggested I stay here like before. I hope you don't mind."

"You can stay here as long as you wish, but you can also come home and stay with me and the children."

He looked at her with surprise. "I didn't know how you were going to react to my visit. You see, I wasn't sure about anything between us, and although your father said you would be happy to see me again, I wasn't sure." He searched her face for an answer, but she simply hugged him more tightly to her own body and led him into her father's house.

Suddenly Ethan felt embarrassed with his wet trunks and tasseled hair and suggested Sarah go swimming while he took a shower and fixed her a mean omelet. There was a catch in his voice when he mentioned the mean omelet. For a minute they both had a flashback to the first time he made her a mean omelet, and they said nothing.

After Sarah had swum to her rock, she lay there for few minutes and closed her eyes. She knew it was a huge surprise to meet Ethan again under such similar circumstance to their first encounter so many years ago, but it had an added patina to it. Ethan was a friend. He was a person she felt comfortable with. She trusted and respected him, and all this after her distasteful encounter with Alex changed the whole picture.

Sarah had no idea why Ethan had come back into her life apart from the fact that he had told her father, he wanted to see her. She didn't know for how long he was going to stay; however, she did know she was happy, and in a peculiar way she felt more secure with Ethan around. She had to admit to herself that since the incident with Alex, she felt a little unsettled; however, she didn't want to go into any other aspects of his visit, so she swam back to her house, took a shower, and changed into a simple summer dress she had kept in her closet many years before.

By the time she walked into the other house, Ethan had already washed and changed into a pair of cut jeans and a faded black T shirt. He looked as young and attractive as she remembered him.

He had laid the table on the porch, which overlooked the white beach and the shimmering sea under the last rays of sun. There were forks and knives, plates, a ball of fresh salad, a pitcher of iced tea, and glasses. He must have done some shopping before he came to the house because there was a loaf of fresh bread and some cheese, and she could smell the wonderful aroma of an omelet with mushrooms and herbs. For a moment she had this feeling of déjà vu again, and it made her smile.

"I hope you are hungry because I am starving." He sat down at the table and put the omelet in front of her. For a moment she felt awkward; however, with the delicious food and her curiosity about Ethan, her appetite won, and they both began eating.

Ethan told her how much he had missed this part of the world and the easy access to the sea. "I hardly ever saw any mass of people on this beach while I was here, and even now, although the weather is still warm, not many beachcombers or swimmers come this direction. Why is that?" he asked.

"When I was a child, my father told me that this beach was notorious because there have been few occurrences of riptide and two people have already lost their lives here." Seeing how Ethan looked at her inquiringly, she elaborated, "A riptide is a head-on collision of conflicting currents, and it can be very dangerous. I remember once I was nearly caught up in a riptide not far from our beach. But luckily my father was next to me, and he directed me not to fight the current but swim around the churning waves. It was a long swim around the cliffs, but that is what saved us."

She looked at him sagely and continued, "You know that reputation is the main part of any tourist pitch, but we are happy there aren't too many visitors on this beach."

"For all it matters, I agree with you." He smiled at her wryly.

Ethan asked about the children, and she told him how sometimes she felt sad and unneeded because all four children had their own individual lives filled with studies, friends, and activities.

"I suppose at some point all parents feel the same like me all over the world. At first our children fill our lives and minds with the care, love, and protection we have to provide them every minute of the day and night. We get involved in every action or movement they engage in. We put our hearts into every grain of pain or laughter they experience, and sometimes even though we may have sometimes wished for some kind of respite from them, it comes as a surprise. Suddenly we are partially redundant and not needed as much as before. They are as independent as Michael and I wished them to be … but too soon." She paused and looked at the sea wistfully and then smiled. "Yes, I suppose they don't need our omnipotent presence around them at all times. But they are just wonderful young human beings, and I love them very much."

Sarah was surprised at her own outburst. She wondered where it had come from. She adored her children and was proud of their individual achievements, their maturity, their inner strength, and the wonderful bond they shared with her and with one another. She surmised the reason was because she had not picked up on her own life and had no partner to share it with. She could see Ethan watching her thoughtfully and changed the subject.

She pulled back some strands of wet hair away from her face and said, "Enough with me and my silly problems. I don't know much about what you do nowadays. The last time I heard anything about you was from my father. You were in Nepal building bridges. Do you still live in the Far East?"

He realized she wasn't comfortable with the unique glimpse she gave him into her personal life but decided to flow with her and accept the change of subject.

"I am engaged at the moment in a gigantic federal project in the United States. I don't suppose you know much about how many bridges there are in the whole of the United States and about their mechanical state. But I can tell you that there are about six hundred thousand bridges there, and according to the latest survey conducted by the federal government, about 11 percent of them need repair or urgent maintenance. This means about sixty-six thousand or more should undergo some kind of major or minor repair. The cost is going to be colossal, something round eighty billions dollars."

Sarah sat riveted to her chair and listened to Ethan's enthusiastic voice tell her about his work. She realized it was one of the only times Ethan had said anything about his work and life away from her. She recalled how very short and intense their time together was when they first met. Ethan had come into her life in a very special junction—graduation from high school, Guy's death, and the initiation into adult life with his expert guidance. It was so very different then.

She looked at Ethan and thought about how subtle the change in him was. He looked the same, but he was different in many ways and had become even more attractive. Now he had some silver strands in his hair. His face was animated, and his body exuded innate strength, a power that showed in the firm line of his jaw, in the disciplined way he moved, and in his deep brown eyes, which sparkled with light coming from the last rays of the setting sun. It was the same Ethan, but he was more mature and more at peace with himself and the world. She noticed he was less tense than before.

"You like what you do, don't you?" she asked casually, and he seemed surprised.

"I love my job."

"What do you actually do in this whole project? It sounds so grand and complicated."

"I don't know if your father ever told you about the engineering firm I founded with a partner about twenty years ago, and although I had been away from the States for long periods of time, I still functioned as the chairman. And later when it became what it is today, one of the most prestigious bridge-building and -maintaining companies in the world, I acted the chief executive of the company." He paused and looked at her inquiringly. "Are you really interested in hearing about my work?"

How could she tell him that she was fascinated with this new facet of his life, this sudden glimpse into his whole world? Up to now she knew nothing but the bare minimal about him. He was about fifty years old, married and divorced once, and he had a son. And now all this information about his successful company and the project of repairing bridges in the United States.

Suddenly it dawned on her how much she missed her daily talks with Michael, how he used to tell her about everything in his work, his ideas for inventions, and his vision of the world in terms of mass communication and electronic gadgets in the future. They used to talk about their children and their concern for their health and dreams. Michael would ask her about her plans for returning to the university and completing her PhD, and she would tell him that the children still needed her full time and there was time to go back to university. And then ... yes, then the whole world collapsed around her, and she had to pick it up and build a new world for herself and her children but without Michael.

Ethan saw her lost in her thoughts and just offered her another glass of ice tea. She declined and quickly pulled herself together.

"I would love to hear everything you want to tell me about your life and work because I don't have the same advantage you have. I don't know much about bridges and surveys on such scales." He looked a little skeptical, so she continued, "I am serious ... really. Would you like to go inside the house, or would you rather sit here?" He nodded with his head, and she volunteered to make a fresh pot of coffee. Sarah stood by the kitchen window and observed Ethan. He looked so close and reachable and yet his face was averted toward the sea. He looked miles away. She wondered where he was and what was going through his mind. Through the open window she said, "A penny for your thoughts." She didn't expect him to answer her but he turned his face to her and gave her that enigmatic smile of his.

"Well, I am thinking about this place, this sea and you. They all take me back to those short and wondrous days so many years ago. It also crossed my mind that I would love you to come and sit next to me so I could feel your warmth and life energy." He paused and kept looking at the expanse of shimmering sea in the horizon. He smiled to himself and returned to look at her. "You know there is still a void between us that we have to resolve, and I have often had misgivings about my behavior with you when you were alone and vulnerable after Guy's death." He crossed his hands on his chest and looked at her resolutely. "And yet I have never regretted what had transpired between us because I consider it as one of the highlights of my life." He was quiet for a moment and then continued, "We both know why I am here now, but I also know that if I want to continue with you anywhere, I will have to win you over in an honorable way. You see, I want you for keeps."

Sarah wanted to say to him that he had already won her over, but she refrained and just brought out into the veranda a tray with new cups, a fresh pot of aromatic coffee together with a box of after eight peppermint chocolates Ethan had brought.

"How about this? Is it good enough for you, kind sir?" She bowed in jest and poured him some hot coffee.

"Be careful. A man could get addicted to such life." He pointed to the sea, to the food, and to her.

"Well, what is stopping you?" Although the question was accompanied with her impish smile, they could both detect a serious strain in her voice. In order to avoid anything further, she said, "Why don't you tell me about your work. I am sincerely interested to know."

"When Peter Gordon and I founded our company, I was in charge of the engineering part, and Peter was in charge of logistics and finance. When I was working in Nepal, I did some surveying for the government, and I found it very useful in my work. So when I returned to work in the States, I suggested we go into independent surveying of bridges and offer them to the government. What happened was that at that point in time, a series of bridges in Washington and Colorado collapsed and cost in life and caused a lot of damage. This alerted the federal government, and a wide scale of surveys is being conducted in the whole of the United States. Hence, the figures I gave you earlier."

He paused and looked at her in amazement. "Are you really interested in what I am telling you?"

For a minute she didn't answer. She was surprised and a little offended. "Do you think I can't grasp what you are telling me or that I am bored with the subject?"

He was quick to correct himself, "Sorry. I didn't mean any disrespect toward your ability to understand what I say. I am simply not used to sharing my thoughts and my work with people who are not in the profession."

"Didn't you ever share your work with your wife or—"

She sensed he was uncomfortable but answered her question anyway. "No, we never discussed anything remotely connected to my work. She once told me it bored her immensely, and since then, I didn't find the occasion to bore any other women." He wasn't looking at her when he said his last words. His eyes were fixed somewhere in the darkening horizon, and there was deep sadness in his eyes.

Sarah felt embarrassed to have witnessed such an intimate glimpse into his private life, so she rose and began clearing up the table. "Would you like to eat or drink anything else before I take everything in?" He got up and started helping her in the kitchen.

They worked as a team, and Sarah recalled how she used to do the same with Michael. It seemed that Ethan was watching her, and he must have seen something in her face. "You miss Michael very much, don't you?" It wasn't so much a question as much as a statement of fact.

"Yes, I do." Sarah's back was turned to him, and she seemed to be lost in memories. "I miss him in so many ways you can't imagine." She paused and then continued, "He used to say that I had brought many shades of light into his life. I think those many shades of light had in fact come from him and illuminated our life. He was the source." She didn't say anything else, and Ethan's heart went out to her.

"Do you have to be home now, or would you care to go for a walk on the beach with me?" he asked. She turned around, and he could see how her eyes sparkled. He just took her arm and led her down to the warm sand and the soothing sound of the sea.

They walked on the beach for a long time, holding hands and not saying much. They both felt the other needed some space to contain the possible change in their lives. Sarah didn't want to think about anything in the future and was content just to hold hands with Ethan and feel his inner strength and calm flow into her body. She knew she desperately needed somebody reliable, strong, and loveable like Ethan beside her to erase the unsavory memory of the barren years from her mind.

They were both walking with bare feet, and they played with the small waves breaking silently onto the beach. Ethan realized how much he had waited for these precious moments with Sarah and how careful he had to be not to make mistakes or take advantage of her vulnerable state of mind.

"I wanted you to know that I might stay here for quite a while. I have spoken to your father, and he has agreed to rent me the house for as long as I wish." He spoke quietly and didn't look at her. "I can do most of my work via my computer or the phone, and my team back home is used to working with me by remote control." He paused and held her back to look at her. "I would like to see you more, if you are not attached to anybody?"

She realized how serious he was and bent her head before she answered, "I am not dating anyone if that is what you mean, and I would love to see more of you." The wind had swept her mass of beautiful hair onto her face, and Ethan had to sweep it all back so that he could read her face.

He loved the touch and texture of her hair, and it pained him not to gather her into his arms and ravish her mouth with kisses and then move to every inch of her body. "Good. So may I take you to dinner in a small and lovely trattoria not far from here this week?" His eyes were sparkling with laughter, and she knew which restaurant he was talking about.

"Yes, I would love to."

"Good. Would you let me know which evening is convenient for you?" Then he kissed her on her head.

They had reached the stairs leading to her home, and he waited for her to gather her things, get into her car, and drive away. He stood there for a long time and somehow knew that he wouldn't have a problem in falling asleep.

Chapter 37

They met in town because Sarah informed him she would not be able get home in time from the office. Ethan was dressed casually with jeans and a pale blue shirt. He was combed and shaved and looked quite handsome. Sarah wore a pair of white linen pants with a deep blue sleeveless silk top, and on it she had a matching white jacket. She looked fresh and elegant with her high-heeled white sandals. He wondered how she could look so enticing and fresh after a day in the office. Her hair was in a ponytail, and she walked straight into his open arms. He could see she was shy with the new situation and just gave her a peck on her lips and walked her into the small and intimate restaurant.

"I remember the last time we were here with your father. Do you come here at all?"

"I have been here a few times with my father, but I don't come often." She paused and then continued, "I suppose I didn't wish to mix between time zones."

"And tonight do you mind us coming here?"

She smiled. "Not at all, we are on a mutual time zone now, and I love the place."

They ordered the chef's specialty of the day—fresh salad, veal escalope, green beans, and mashed potatoes. A bottle of red Chianti helped them relax and feel free with each other.

She knew from the past how easy it was to talk to Ethan. He always added some fresh look on any topic they discussed and possessed sharp, self-effacing humor. Sarah asked him about his friend the archeologist, Dr. Robin Ford, and he laughed. "You wouldn't believe it. Whenever we meet or talk on the phone, he asks me about you and can't stop praising your beauty and poise. Well, you have one loyal admirer roaming the world. Would you believe it that he has already divorced his fourth wife? They are lovely to look at first, but they become dull and boring after a short while. It is never his fault in choosing them."

Sarah asked him about his son, and his face lit up. "Erran is just wonderful. Despite the failure of our marriage, he has managed to keep his relationships with both his mother and me as pleasant as possible. He is mature for his twenty-six years. He graduated his law studies from Georgetown University in Washington and has finished his internship with a big law firm in the capital. He has a lovely girlfriend and intends to marry her." His face was animated, and he looked very happy speaking about his boy. "I would like you to meet him sometime. I think you would like him."

"Well, if he is anything like his father, then I already like him."

They both smiled.

The food was as delicious as they remembered it from the past, and Ethan said it was one of the best restaurants he had eaten in. "I can tell you that if this trattoria were anywhere in New York or Washington, it would be packed. I am also sure the company I keep has a lot to say for the place too." He poured her some more wine, and then he suggested, "I love jazz music, and looking at the newspapers, I found that a very famous and interesting band I knew during my college years is performing here in town on Friday night. Would you like to join me?" He could discern some discomfort in her eyes.

"I love jazz bands, and Michael and I used to go to jazz sessions quite often. But I thought of inviting you to join me and the children on Friday evening for dinner. You see, it is a tradition with us to get together once a week, and so I could introduce you to them." He was surprised a little but figured it was the best way to break the ice with her family.

"I would love to join you all for dinner. The jazz session is very late, so maybe we can do both."

She was relived. "Yes, that would be wonderful."

Chapter 38

Ethan had sent a beautiful bouquet of flowers to her home before he arrived there for the first time. He had also brought a big box of chocolates and a bottle of excellent wine.

The children were all present, and Ethan was deeply impressed with their good looks, their poise, and the uncanny bond among them. They seemed to communicate with each other without much talk, and they all adored their mother. They all stood up to shake his hand when he walked into the lovely family room. It smelled of home-cooked food and was lit with many white candles. It looked homely and festive at the same time.

The eldest, who resembled Michael in everything but for his eyes, was Tom, and he approached Ethan with a stretched hand. "I am Tom. It is nice to meet you, sir, and these are my siblings." They all shook hands with him, and he held his breath when the little one, Laura, shook his hand. She was the spitting image of Sarah when she was young, with the same bounty of beautiful chestnut hair, gray eyes, and budding feminine figure.

It was Tom who asked him, "Did you know our father?"

Sarah held her breath and regretted not telling the children more about their visitor; however, Ethan had the presence of mind and directed his answer to the boy. "I was lucky to have met your father a few times in the States." He didn't look at Sarah but continued, "My father and your grandfather Joe used to be friends when they were young, and your grandfather has been coming to the States for years. He once introduced me to your father when he came to New York on business, and since then I met him several times in different places." He paused and looked at all the children. "Your father was a fine man, and I regret not to have known him better. I am sorry for your loss."

The children looked at him solemnly for a moment, evaluating what he had said. Then Sarah defused the tense moment and suggested they all sit down to dinner. It was Laura who said, "You must meet our nanny, Dora. She is the most important member of the family after Mummy."

Dora looked much more mature and happier than the first time she came to live with the family. She looked at Ethan shyly and seemed to sense the undercurrents between him and Sarah. "I am delighted to meet you, and I hope you like the food."

"I am delighted to meet you, and I can't wait to eat your food." Ethan bent and kissed both her cheeks to the delight of the children.

The food was excellent, and everybody seemed to be in a good mood. There was beef stew, fried chicken, meatballs in tomato sauce, rice, baked potatoes, different kinds of fresh green beans, some spaghetti bolognas, and lots of water jugs. The grown-ups had wine glasses too.

Throughout the meal the older children teased the younger ones, and young Arik retaliated by disclosing a sensational secret about his older brother. He suddenly said, "Tom, can I tell Mummy about your girlfriend?"

Tom gave him a warning look, and they all burst out giggling and laughing. Sarah interfered by chiding the younger boy.

"We don't tell secrets even if we are teased. Anyway, I am sure Tom will introduce her to us when he is ready."

She looked at all of them and saw how Arik whispered a silent "sorry" to Tom, and the others just smiled at him.

Ethan had a wonderful time with this incredible family. He was impressed with Dona's sharp mind and how both she and her twin followed his explanations about the bridge project he was engaged in back in the United States. He was asked how he managed his work when he was away from his office. He told them about the newest developments in electronic communications, and here Tom and Dona amazed him with their up-to-date knowledge about what their father's company dealt with and how they envisioned the future.

At one point he turned to Sarah and said, "You didn't tell me you have two computer geniuses at home. So who is going to continue in your father's line of work?"

"We both are." Tom and Dona looked at each other and laughed. They all laughed and Laura said, "We are twins, but we are one mind split into two, right, Mummy?"

"It seems like it," she said and continued, "You see, Ethan, although I have four children, I only have to deal with two. If I speak to one, the other knows it immediately and complies."

Ethan sat back and looked at all of them. "You are an amazing family, and I congratulate your mother on doing such a great job with the lot of you."

They all beamed at him with satisfaction. "Do you have children?" It was little Laura again, and Ethan looked at her without being aware how bewitched he was with the young girl.

"I have a son who practices law in Washington."

She only said, "Oh." And smiled at him impishly like her mother.

It was Tom who asked him whether he was in the same business as his grandfather Joe.

"No, I build bridges, and at the moment I am involved in a big federal project in the United States that deals with surveying structurally deficient bridges and trying to repair them." Sarah could see he had captured their imagination and how they looked at him in owe. "If you wish, I can show you some fantastic pictures of amazing bridges in the United States and the world."

They were being served tea and coffee, and the smell of Sarah's apple cake filled the house. Ethan gave a big sigh and asked, "What is this wonderful smell coming from the kitchen?"

"You must eat Mummy's strudel. She got the receipt from Grandma Rachel. It is really delicious."

"Well, if you, Laura, recommend it, then I am bound to love it."

He smiled at Sarah, who was beaming at her children.

"She is also a good cook," Laura went on, "but she bakes best because Dora is the best cook too."

She became aware she had gone too far, and Arik replied instead of her, "After you taste it, you would like an extra helping."

"Well, I am sure to do so," said Ethan.

But then Arik asked hesitantly while he was looking at his twin, "Laura wants to know if the chocolates you brought are only for mother?"

The big ones looked at the younger twins reproachfully, and Sarah looked at them with stormy eyes. She knew they were in cahoots, but Ethan glanced in her direction and intervened with, "They are for all of you."

After all the children had eaten their portion of chocolates and cakes, Sarah told the younger twins they had double duty in the kitchen instead of the older twins. "That will teach you when and what to say around the dinner table." The twins didn't object in any way but quietly discussed between them what each would do. Ethan could see it was a regular occurrence and just smiled at Sarah. For a moment there was some whispering between Dona and her mother. Then she asked Ethan if he would like to visit their father's company. "You see, Tom and I spend at least one day a week at the plant, and we would like to show you what we do."

Ethan was surprised, and after he saw Sarah's nod and the twins' expectant faces, he said, "I would be more than honored to see what you two are planning for our future. Thank you for the offer."

On the way to the club Sarah was pensive, and Ethan guessed what was on her mind. "I am sorry not to have mentioned to you the fact that I had met Michael a few times. In fact, I was sure you knew about it."

"No, I didn't know anything about it, and my father didn't mention it either. I wonder why Michael said nothing to me. Normally he would tell me about new people he had met, especially if they were introduced by Dad." She thought about it a little more and then said, "I suppose Michael made the connection between us somehow. He was very astute and intuitive to body language and emotional undercurrents, so he might have guessed the identity of the mystery man from my past and decided not to bring it up."

"For all it matters, I can tell you he was a hell of a guy. He was sharp, astute, and very bright. I can see him in the older twins." He turned to look at her and carried on. "You have the most wonderful family I have seen in a long time. You have done a marvelous job with them, and I salute you."

"Well, I didn't do it alone. I had Michael in their formative years, and then Dora and the grandparents deserve a big credit too." She smiled wryly. "Don't forget their genes."

"No, I can never forget where they have come from. I think in the case of your children, nature and nurture have done a great job together."

Chapter 39

The club was dimly lit and nearly full. Ethan had booked them a table in advance, so he ordered their drinks, and they sat at a dark corner table on soft cushions with a good view of the stage. Sarah knew Ethan would remember her favorite drink and relished the first sip of the gin and tonic with ice. Ethan was nursing his neat whiskey, and his hand was wrapped around her shoulders. Sarah felt how the alcohol was releasing the tension of the whole week and the evening with the children out of her body.

"I am glad my children like you. I wasn't sure about it, not because of you but for the fact that I have never brought any unknown guests for Friday dinners." She paused, and Ethan just looked at her and let her go on. "It is important for me."

He kissed her neck and tightened his arm around her shoulders. "It is very important for me too. You see, if I want to woo you successfully, I must have the children on my side." His eyes were twinkling, and he was smiling.

"Are you planning on wooing me seriously?"

"Am I not doing it properly?"

"How long are you going to carry on with this formal wooing?"

"Until I feel I deserve you." He looked into her eyes expectantly, and she seemed to grasp all the words he wasn't saying about the first time they met.

"I don't regret a moment of what we experienced the first time we met. In fact, I owe you a great debt, and you shouldn't feel bad about it." Sarah looked at him in earnest, and he simply pulled her closer and kissed her lips.

"You see, I don't regret a single moment of those incredible short summer days together with you too. They are some of the most cherished moments of my life. But you have been single for a long time, and I would like to date you and ply you with wine and roses and then … ravish you."

She started giggling and said, Promises, promises."

The people around them were a mixture of all ages—some very young, some very old, and a lot in their mid-forties and fifties. Sarah knew some of the faces, and she was sure they would wonder about Ethan next to her. She just nodded her head to them.

Ethan told her that the jazz band they were about to hear was well known all around the world. The ensemble was inspired by the tradition of the famous Royal Society Jazz Orchestra with ten gifted musicians and an incredibly gifted singer named Carla Normand. She not only looked like Billie Holiday but sang like her too. She had a warm, rich voice and sang with confidence and emphasis on the lyrics and the nuances of the composer's craft. It was difficult to select a highlight from the band's repertoire because every song was unique in itself and it seemed to have captured the minds and hearts of the audience.

Sarah and Ethan felt elated; however, it was way past midnight, and Ethan could feel how tired Sarah was. Just as the band finished its extended session and took a break, they left the club, and Ethan took her home.

"I am going to be away for the whole week at least, but I shall return for sure. I would like to suggest something."

She looked at him inquiringly. "What do you suggest?"

"If you don't mind, I would like you, Dora, and the children to go out with me on the first Friday night after I return to an open-bar restaurant on the beach. We can all have fun, and nobody would have to cook or clean up after us. It is a good restaurant, and there is a variety of dishes."

She thought for a minute and then said, "I think it would be a lovely change, but first let me put it to the children and Dora. They all have to agree."

When they reached her home, he took her to the door, gave her a deep kiss and drove away once she got in.

Ethan noticed that Sarah didn't ask him where he was going and why. This was one of Sarah's most endearing features, and he appreciated her more for it. He knew he had to attend to few matters in his office in New York and bring back with him some personal stuff if he wished to stay here longer.

After she checked on the children, Sarah fell asleep quite fast. She was tired and not used to drinking so much alcohol in one evening. The next day, however, she thought about the meal, the jazz session, and Ethan's insistence on wooing her "formally," as he had put it, and she just giggled.

I wonder what he has in store for me, she thought.

The children, on the other hand, told her how much they liked Ethan and how cool it was that he knew their father. It was Tom who expressed their inner thoughts. "I am sure he would be amazed when he sees father's plant and what Dona and I are working on. Maybe it could help him with his bridges." Sarah felt how her heart went out to her grown children who missed Michael in so many different ways.

"Ethan told me that once he returns from his trip, he would fix a date with you two to visit the plant. By the way, he suggested that all you guys together with Dora and I go dine with him on Friday evening in a restaurant. What do you say?" They all cheered the idea and said it would be cool to dine out like grown-ups.

Sarah called Ethan and offered to take him to the airport, and he was very grateful. They had time to have coffee before his flight was announced, and just before boarding started, he took her in his arms and inhaled the fresh smell of her hair and felt her body melt into his. They stood quietly in each other's arms, and he whispered into her ear, "I promise to be back as soon as possible, and this time I shall stay much longer. You know I haven't finished courting you yet." She felt him smile in her hair and half-cried and half-smiled back.

"Don't you dare not come back, Ethan Saddot. I have a crowd of hungry children who are waiting for you to arrive, so I feed them and their nanny too. So—"

He kissed her eyes and said, "I'll be back, sweetheart, because I want you and I need you. Don't go away." He gave her a long kiss and walked toward the departure entrance.

Chapter 40

Ethan called nearly every day from wherever he was and informed her about what he was doing. Apparently the pile of work he had expected was much bigger and demanded more time than he had allocated for it. He had to attend to his home and visit his son in Washington, DC. He sounded very happy and energized. "You can't imagine how much I am looking forward to returning back to you," he said to her, and she told him about the children and their reaction to his offer of dinner outside. He was delighted.

"I have asked one of the assistants here to prepare a set of pictures of the bridges our company has repaired and some beautiful pictures of unique bridges in the United States. I think the older twins will appreciate them."

"I am sure they will love them and consider them very cool." They both laughed. "I miss you," she whispered into the phone and heard him hold his breath.

Then he whispered back, "I miss you too, sweetheart, and I hope to make up my absence to you when I return." He blew her a kiss and got off the line.

Ethan contacted Sarah's father to ask whether he could rent the house on a permanent basis so he could move some of his office and personal stuff there. Once he got Joe's blessings, he decided to open an affiliate office in the house. He then flew to Washington to visit his son and be with him for a couple of days.

Erran was about twenty-six years old, and he was of medium size and very fair. He had his father's athletic gait when he walked and his generous mouth, but he took mainly after his Nordic mother, with blue eyes and very fair hair. Ethan was excited to see him settled in his law firm and content with his work. It was quite clear to see how father and son loved and appreciated each other and were happy to meet again. Ethan embraced him warmly, and Erran patted his father on his shoulder and then held him away from him for a minute and said, "You look different, Dad. You look younger. Have you found yourself a new love?" Ethan, though surprised to hear his son's unexpected observation said, "An old love."

"Good for you, Dad. I would love to meet her someday soon."

"Yes, of course, someday soon," he replied but began talking about Erran and his plans to get married to Mary, his girlfriend.

Ethan was flooded with memories of scenes with Sarah and the children and felt an almost physical need to embrace them and hear their young voices. He knew he loved Erran and was proud of him, but his heart was with Sarah and her children, who were a wonderful and unexpected bonus. He saw his son watching him closely but refrained from saying anything else about the change in him.

Erran introduced his father to his colleagues, many of whom had heard of his remarkable work with the federal bridge project. Some of the partners and associates in the firm shook hands with him and commented about how bright and promising Erran was, and Ethan beamed with pride. In the evening after he had gone to his hotel, washed, and changed clothes, he called Sarah and told her about meeting Erran.

"Do you know what the first thing Erran said to me was?" He paused and gave a small chuckle. "He said I looked different and younger."

"For your information," Sarah said, "Dona caught me singing in the house, and she, too, said I looked happy. I suppose they are right, and we have wonderful children."

Ethan had booked a table in a small French restaurant on the Potomac for the three of them, and the meal was delicious. He liked Mary at once. She looked very different from Erran. She told him she was half Indian American and half German. She was very slim with long black hair and lovely mocha chocolate complexion. The amazing things about her were her brilliant green eyes. She was beautiful, and Erran seemed to be deeply in love with her. Mary worked for the government in the justice department and met Erran at university. They intended to get married the following spring, and Ethan promised to attend it.

"With your new paramour, I hope," Erran said and then told Mary how Ethan had found an "old-new" love and why he looked so good. Ethan felt how he was blushing and decided not to elaborate on the subject in any way. He was not ready to speak about Sarah with anybody yet, so he raised his wine glass and drank to their health.

He spent the next day with Mary and Erran going to the Smithsonian Science Museum, where he bought special gifts for the younger twins. Next they went to the renovated Union Train Station with all its coffee bars and shops and spent the evening in a musical and a meal in an Indonesian restaurant. He flew back to New York the next morning, and at lunchtime he was on a flight again.

Chapter 41

Sarah made it her custom to go swimming at least twice a week after she finished her work in the plant and if the children didn't need her. Sometimes when it was quite late, she would call in to her home and tell Dora to go on with supper for the children.

She was in her shower, singing while shampooing her hair after the long swim in the sea. It wasn't an easy job to wash her mass of hair and rinse it under a torrent of water, so it was no wonder she didn't hear the doorbell ring or the front door open and shut quietly.

Ethan had arrived a short while before, and he was thrilled to see Sarah's car in her drive and hear her singing in the shower. The first thing he wanted to do was to slip into the shower and hold her under the running water and kiss her for all the hours and days he had missed her, but he didn't. It reminded him of Hitchcock's film *Psycho*, and he knew how frightened she would be. He also recalled the night in the pond after Guy's death and how frightened Sarah had been when he had lifted her out of the water. He decided to wait for her, so when she finally finished and came out of the shower cubical, he held a big towel in his hands and saw how genuinely happy she was to see him.

"Ethan, you have come back." She was so happy to see him that she gasped in surprise and walked right toward his open arms, but in the same minute she became aware of her dripping, naked body and halted in embarrassment. It took her a moment to make up her mind that Ethan had seen her naked body and that it was more urgent to embrace him and ease the gnawing pain in her heart and her loins than to be coy with him.

She could see that though he was fully dressed, Ethan was fully aroused from just looking at her. He looked at her graceful body and just held his breath. He had carried her image in his mind for more than thirty years. She was simply part of him. He closed his eyes for a moment and could feel her supple limbs entwined around him and her wet hair engulfing him like an aromatic waterfall. She was dripping water, and her lovely gray eyes were glistening. Her full lips were parted. She was beckoning him to approach her, but his eyes were glued to her full breasts. Her body had not changed much after all these years. She still had a slim figure, and her beautiful long legs joined at the dark thatch of hair in her pelvis, where he focused his whole attention now.

He knew it was a matter of seconds before he ravished her whole body and satiated his thirst for her, but he had promised himself not to rush her and take it easy.

He wrapped her in the big towel and held her close to his body. She held his head in her hands and kissed him. They kissed for a long time while his hands tried to dry different parts of her body. She would not let him stop the kiss, and he had to twist his arms and legs around her gyrating torso to reach her hidden parts. At last they both had to stop kissing and come up for air, and he caught her mass of dripping hair in the towel, trying to dry it. At the same moment with one fluid movement, Sarah draped her thighs around his waist and wrapped her naked body around him.

It was a short walk to her bed, and she laid her wet body on top of his dry clothes with the wet towel between them. He was content to have her in his arms for as long as she wanted, while she was savoring his special smell and the strength of his muscles beneath her. After a while Sarah slipped off the bed and pulled the towel around her.

"I am sorry for this wild welcome, but you surprised me."

"I am very happy with your welcome and would wish for it every time we meet," he said, and she giggled like a schoolgirl.

"I ruined your clothes," she said shyly.

"Yes, but you also put out some of the fire burning in me." He jumped off the bed and put his arms on her shoulders. "Are you free this evening, and can I come and see the kids?"

"Tom and Dona are studying and will be home quite late, but Laura and Arik are at home."

"Can I join you at home after I unpack and take a proper shower?"

She smiled and went on to wear her underwear and a green cotton dress and then combed her unruly hair. She sat on a chair and held the hair dryer in her hand while Ethan brushed her hair back. He told her how he always wanted to do it, and she leaned her head back and let him kiss her eyes and lips.

He came after an hour, all fresh and dry. The children jumped with joy to see him. He presented them with their private gifts of astronaut food and drink, and each received a package filled with chocolates.

They were all over him with thanks and took him to their rooms to show him their school projects and private collections.

Sarah had prepared a light meal and called Ethan to join her. They sat down to eat after all the commotion with the young twins had died down. The children hugged him and went to their rooms.

Tom and Dona arrived together in their joint car. They were both happy to see him, and Tom shook his hand while Dona simply kissed him on his cheek. Sarah could see that Ethan was emotionally moved with the children's reaction toward him. She was happy and proud of them and realized how he was happy to be welcomed by them and to feel at home.

"Can you make it to the plant this week? We are in a tricky mechanical stage and would be happy to talk to you about it." It was Dona who asked him, and Tom explained they had come up with an idea for a chip that would help handicapped people operate extra facets in their own wheelchairs.

Ethan said he would be delighted and fixed a date with both of them in the plant. When he gave them the sets of beautiful panoramic pictures of bridges, they were thrilled. Each got a different set, and after they thanked him profusely, they retired to their rooms. Sarah watched the interaction between the older twins and Ethan with avid interest and sensed a deep feeling of gratitude. She knew she was blessed.

Ethan had become a regular visitor to the house, and all the children felt free to call him and discuss with him what Ethan called "adolescent and man stuff." They often told him about what they used to do with Michael, and in return, he told them about Erran and the hiking trips they used to take in the mountains and to the small bridges in the countryside.

Chapter 42

One evening after they all had dinner together and the children had left them alone in the living room, Ethan asked whether she would go with him to a hotel lodge in the north for a weekend. Sarah was surprised but agreed gladly. She told him they had to wait for a couple of weeks, as Michael's parents were celebrating their fiftieth wedding anniversary and Sarah was giving a special dinner party with Joe and Ruth, and even Ben was due from London with his family.

Sarah was aware of the strain it would put on Ethan to meet Michael's family for the first time, but it was time they all met him. The children had spoken about him a lot, and she knew they were anxious and curious about the man who seemed to have taken the place of their son in Sarah and the children's lives.

The occasion was very festive, and all the guests were excited and jolly. The house was brightly lit, and there was a sumptuous display of flowers, food, and drinks. Sarah's father introduced Ethan to Rachel, Jack, and Ben and informed them about his own ties with Ethan's father since their air force days. He told them about Ethan's involvement in the big bridge project repair and renovation in the United States and suggested they see the pictures in the twins' rooms.

They were all impressed with his credentials and affable manners. It was clear the children liked him very much, and there was a good bond between him and Sarah. At one point Rachel asked, "Where did Michael meet Ethan, Sarah?"

And just before Sarah had time to answer, it was Joe, Sarah's father, who answered instead, "Michael and Ethan first met through me. Once when I met Michael in New York, Ethan was in the same hotel, so I made the introductions." He turned to Ethan and said, "You told me you had met Michael few more times, didn't you?"

Ethan immediately replied, "Yes, he was a great guy, and I am sorry for your loss." They all kept quiet, and Ethan continued, "I met Sarah when I came here to visit Joe." At that point Joe took Rachel and Jack to see the older children's rooms.

Sarah could see that Ben had come with an open mind and accepted Ethan's presence in the house with equanimity. He caught Sarah in the kitchen and whispered in her ear, "You could do worse, sister-in-law. He is not bad at all." She blushed slightly, and he gave her a small peck on her cheek.

Ethan had booked them in a small wooden bungalow that was part of a big compound with some other bungalows and a central hall that served as a lobby and a dining hall. Each bungalow comprised of a small living room that opened to a large bedroom with a huge double bed. The color scheme of the furniture and drapery in the suite was in blue and beige. The main attraction of the bungalow was the private outdoor Jacuzzi which overlooked a dense forest. The whole place was in the middle of a wooded region, and everything was rustic and very peaceful. There was a small pond that one could see from the dining hall and a few paths leading into the thick wood and up the mountains. They met very few guests while they registered in the lobby, and then they went for a short hike after they left their suitcases and changed into some outdoor clothes in their bungalow.

Ethan had informed himself of the different attractions of the place, and they walked along a wide path, holding hands and smiling. The wood was cool and the smell of the pines was refreshing. It had a mixture of pine trees, and in between there were the lovely poplar trees with their rustling dual-color leaves. Sarah noticed how elegant the poplars were, and it seemed to her they were all whispering secrets to the pine trees.

It was an easy incline, and they hardly felt the climb up. After a while they reached a clearing, and they could see their hotel lodges and the pond all lying in front of them in the valley below. It was a beautiful view, and they stood there holding each other's hand and soaking the magic tranquility of the place.

"I thought you were going to take me to the hotel with the lake, where we had stayed after we had met Robin and his archeological dig."

She turned to look at him, and he looked at her with thoughtful eyes and said, "I did consider it at first, but as I told you before, I want a clean start for both of us."

On the way down they met some other guests and walked to the main lobby to have coffee with them. They were told that there was going to be a small concert of a cappella singers later in the evening. After a while Sarah suggested they retire to their room to refresh themselves before dinner and entertainment. Sarah changed into a pair of worn-out jeans with a fresh white T-shirt, and Ethan wore nearly the same but asked her to precede him to the dining hall, as he still had to shave.

The couple they had befriended had two free seats at their round table, so Sarah and Ethan joined them gladly. She was a high school biology teacher, and he owned an import-export firm of medical parts. The food was quite simple but delicious, and they all drank beer. The conversation was about the couple's two grown-up children and work, but they mainly talked about the lodge and its merits. "We have been coming here for years on the same date, and we have never been disappointed," said the man, and his wife beamed with pride.

Ethan joined in with, "It looks promising, and we hope to have a good time." They introduced themselves by their names without any further details.

They were both delighted and surprised with the quality of the singers in the little lobby after the meal. A cappella music is normally church music sung in a mixed group of male and female singers without being accompanied by any instruments. This group was comprised of five young women and four young men, and their conductor was a lady in her late sixties who seemed to be a big source of inspiration for her singers. They sang a mixture of lovely Renaissance and Baroque music.

Chapter 43

Sarah and Ethan were embracing each other and laughing when they walked into their dimly lit lodge. The first thing Sarah noticed in the dim bedroom was a medium-sized square box beautifully wrapped with shimmering pink paper and lovely ribbons on her bed. She looked at Ethan, and he nodded with his head. "It is for you," he said.

She was surprised and delighted. It was the first time that Ethan had given her anything personal, and Sarah didn't know what to expect. Ethan lay on the bed with his hands behind his head and simply looked at her. "I am not going to tell you what is in it, so you'd better open it," he urged her.

Sarah sat on the edge of the bed and slowly opened the box. It contained a magical set of satin and lace lingerie. She gasped with surprise and delight. There was a beautiful pair of pale satin panties with lacey borders. She held them in her hands without looking at Ethan and blushed slightly. Next came out a satin bra with French designed rose lace exactly her size. She looked at him inquiringly, and he said, "I still remember something about you." She went on to dig out the most wonderful satin camisole with French designed rose lace. At last came out a long and exquisite dressing gown with the same motives of the rest of the garments.

Sarah held it to herself and gasped with joy. "It is all so beautiful and soft to touch." She looked at him with sparkling eyes.

"You had better put it on at least for few minutes before I take it off myself. I have been waiting for this moment for a long time."

She got off the bed and slowly began taking off her jeans, her T-shirt, her bra, and her panties. Her body was curvy and sensuous. Ethan took a deep breath and wondered how magnificent and desirable she looked. Sarah began to put on her new lingerie with seductive movements and each time looked for his approval.

After she had put on the gorgeous dressing gown, she curtsied gracefully. For a moment Ethan seemed to be riveted to the bed, but suddenly he jumped off the bed and lifted her up in the air.

"Please help me take off all the satin before I tear them off myself," he said while his hands were in frenzy and his mouth was guzzling her lips and face.

Sarah simply wriggled out of the lace and satin garments and wrapped herself around Ethan while he quickly discarded his own clothes on the floor and kept kissing her. Sarah was acutely aware of Ethan's arousal pushing into her pelvis. Ethan carried her to the bed and lay alongside her voluptuous and enticing body. He spread his fingers in her long, beautiful hair and kissed her mouth till she had to come up for breath. His caressing hands moved to her face, neck, and breasts and then began dancing with the two ripe globs of her breast. He took the nipples in his mouth in turn and covered her whole body with passionate kisses.

Sarah's hands caressed and kneaded his shoulders, arms, chest, and abdomen with feverish fingers. She lifted each of his buttocks and grounded her pelvis onto them. Her hands finally reached his crotch and fondled his swollen balls and formidable erection. Ethan groaned and moaned, and at the same time he sought her mouth again while his fingers separated the swollen lips of her vagina and entered it with delicate probing. He reached her clitoris, and Sarah emitted a guttural moan of pleasure and led him into her core.

They made love for long hours, and for the time they satiated their thirst and need for each other. Ethan was generous with his desire to please her and answer her needs; however, Sarah was not a young and inexperienced woman who needed guidance anymore. She rewarded him with a more mature approach and expertise. She flirted and seduced him with various affectionate and sensual teasing. She whispered sweet sounds and murmurs in his ears, and when he took a short respite from his arduous labors, she woke him up with languid strokes and soft caresses.

At one point he lay next to her on the bed and looked into her glowing face and said, "I want you to know that I have loved you from the first moment I saw you on the beach in your father's house, and I shall love you as long as I live." His declaration of commitment and love was so sincere that Sarah had tears in her eyes.

Sarah was equally sincere when she said, "My dear, dear lover and friend, I love you and shall love you for as long as you wish me to."

Ethan pushed a wisp of stray hair behind her ear, took her face in his hands, and said, "Would you let me be your man for as long as we both wish?"

She smiled tenderly, kissed him, and buried her face in his body.

Chapter 44

Older Sarah

Ethan had kept his promise to me, and we have been together for all these years. They have been years filled with passion, love, and pleasure. They were also laced with age.

We have had our separate memories and recollections of experiences and people, but we have also forged a deep bond between us and our families. My children have been thrilled to have Ethan as my partner in life and as their guardian angel. They love and respect him and see in his son, Erran, a big brother and part of our family.

Ethan lived with me and the children in our home most of the time. However, as years have passed, the children left one by one. Some years ago Ethan bought my father's house for work and retreat. My children are all grown up and married. I have many grandchildren, and to my delight, great-grandchildren are on the way.

Lately Ethan has moved to his house on the beach, and I stay in mine, which is attached to his villa. We spend many hours together; however, Ethan spends more hours in his own beach house because of his failing health, and then I go and stay with him.

We left the big house for the children. Ethan hasn't been all that well lately, and he needs more quiet and peace; however, our lives been twined together for so long that even when we are apart for a few hours, we are together, and I see in him my better half.

I have become aware that Ariel has been visiting me only when Ethan does not spend the night with me, and it has crossed my mind that it is Ethan himself who sends Ariel to keep me company. I have often told Ethan about Ariel, and he always smiles as he listens to me talk about him.

Ethan has been sleeping peacefully next to me all night, and I wonder why I suddenly sense Ariel in my bedroom. He hovers over my body, touches my face and hair, and then kisses me on my lips before he dissolves in the morning mist coming through the window. The room is very peaceful and quiet, and I realize that Ethan is no longer sleeping peacefully beside me.

(Ms. Shoshana Avni) July 2014